DEATH COMES IN THREES

AN ADDIE FOSTER MYSTERY

Kimberley O'Malley

Carolina Blue
PUBLISHING

Published by Carolina Blue Publishing, LLC

ISBN: 978-1-946682-10-9

In memory of Joan Ann Stanton, 25 April 1938-29 July 2018

I was deep into my contemporary romance series when I lost my Mom to Alzheimer's. And I had to stop. That book deals too heavily with grief. I just couldn't do it. The idea for a Cozy series had been lurking in my brain for months. I wasn't sure when I would have the time to write it. And then I knew. So, this very first of my new series, my new genre, is dedicated to the best mom ever. She always told me I could do anything that I set my mind to. And she was right. I miss you every day.

Chapter One

Sweat dotted her brow and upper lip. She twisted away, desperate to escape his grasp. "No," Addie cried, but the word fell on deaf ears. His maniacal grin shone in the dark. His laugh echoed in the empty room. She didn't know where she was. Couldn't see her captor's eyes. But her heart galloped in her chest like a wild horse. She had to break free of him. If she could just escape. Suddenly, she was falling through the darkness, not escaping so much as plummeting to her death.

Addie gasped as she landed with a thud. And struggled to break free of her bonds. Her blue eyes popped open. The familiar sunny yellow walls of her bedroom comforted her. Four concerned eyes stared at her. She reached out to pet two silky heads. Her Shelties, Gracey and Lily, licked her hand. She kicked at her comforter, freeing her legs from the tangled mess. She was on the floor of her bedroom, not in a dark and scary room. She took a deep breath as the thudding of her heart subsided. Yet she could still taste the metallic bite of fear on her tongue.

Sighing, she sat up, leaning against the bed. She reached into the drawer of her bedside table. Grabbing her spiral notebook, she jotted down the details that remained fresh in her mind. As she scribbled, "Fun, Fun, Fun" by the Beach Boys sounded from her phone. Her BFF's favorite past time was to change her ring tone. She answered it, continuing to make notes.

"Yes?"

"Adelaide Foster, were you planning on coming in today? Or should I just soldier on without you?"

The sound of his sarcastic tone grounded her. She glanced at the phone for the time. Ten o'clock! Addie never missed her alarm. "I have no idea what happened, Grey." She held her breath. Greyson Waverly may be her best and oldest friend, but mornings weren't his thing. He wasn't civil until she plied him with his caffeine choice of the day. Usually a triple, foamy, over the top sweet something. "Give me thirty minutes. I'll bring caffeine. I promise."

"Oh, honey. Did you have another bad dream?" Sympathy oozed across the distance between them.

"Yes," she whispered.

"Are you writing it down?"

Her heart clutched. No one got her the way he did. "As we speak."

"Okay, then. You are granted an additional five minutes. I'll text you my order."

She stared at the now silent phone and laughed. Until tears rolled down her cheeks. She might be going nuts, but Grey would always be there for her. Would always be able to make her laugh.

Lily tilted her head, as if trying to figure out what Addie was doing. She reached out and ruffled her silky ears with the fingers of one hand. Gracey, not to be outdone, walked into Addie's open arms, resting her head on her human's shoulder in silent support.

"It's okay, girls. Mommy's fine." She hoped that was true. For over a week, she'd been having these weird dreams. Each time, the same nameless, faceless man threatened her. The setting changed. But the all-consuming terror did not. Each time, she awoke with a vague sense of unease. Like something bad was about to happen. Each time, that sense grew. But there were never specifics. Just a feeling of doom.

Lily yipped once, sharp and to the point. That was her 'I have to go' bark. "Okay, let's go potty." Both dogs turned and ran, their nails clicking on the hardwood floor of her bedroom. She got up slower than them, wincing as she rubbed her lower back. She wasn't twenty anymore, and that fall was going to leave a bruise.

She hobbled into the kitchen, dodging the eight paws, and opened the back slider. The girls raced outside. The fenced in yard may be small, but it was their domain. They would be busy for a while, first attending to their needs and then sniffing every blade of grass. Only when they were sure no marauding cat, or raccoon, had invaded their territory would they return to the slider.

Satisfied they were otherwise occupied, Addie took a quick shower. She was cutting into her allotted thirty-five minutes, but showering was her caffeine. Grey would have to wait. If for no other reason, she needed to remove the sweat. If only washing away the lingering fear proved so easy. She turned the water to just short of boiling and stood under the spray, allowing the water to work its magic.

Another not so lovely side effect of the dreams were the headaches. Sometimes a dull ache settled at the base of her skull. Other times, blinding pain throbbed between her eyes. Today's fell into the first category. She shampooed her hair, concentrating on massaging her fingertips into said base of skull. She could have stood there for another hour, but the clock was ticking. She rinsed the shampoo, threw in a leave in conditioner, washed and rinsed her body, and cut off the water.

"Dang it," she muttered. She'd forgotten the fan. Thick, foggy steam swirled throughout the small room, lowering visibility to next to nothing. Slowing her down. Grey was going to kill her. She swiped a hand across the mirror, squinting at her reflection. Dark circles underlined her eyes. There wasn't enough concealer in the world to fix that, not that she had time for make-up. *Tick Tock.* She threw some product in her hair, grateful as always for her curls, and dashed into her closet. Pulling the nearest thing she could reach off its hanger, she slid the cotton T-shirt over her head and pulled on a pair of capris. Plucking espadrilles from the hopeless tangle of shoes on the floor of her closet, she slipped them on as she headed back into the kitchen.

Opening the slider, she whistled for the girls. They came at a run, wrapping their sunshine-warmed bodies around her legs. Knowing as only dogs could that breakfast was due, they danced at her feet, tongues lolling from their mouths. "Yes, girls, I know your belly thinks your throats have been cut. Let's go to work."

At the magic word, Lily and Gracie raced to the front door. Tails held up like flags, they whined and yipped.

"I should be so excited to go to work every day." She clipped their leashes onto their collars and grabbed her purse and keys. "Let's do this, before Grey gets any madder at me." She smiled to herself, knowing that Grey's moods were all bluff. The two had been friends since single digits. And caffeine cured everything.

She stepped outside and turned to lock the door. As she held open the storm door with her hip, one of the dogs pulled on their leash, causing her to lose her balance. Gracey was a flash of gray and black as she raced off the porch and down the sidewalk. Lily, her sister and the calmer of the two, whined. She pressed against Addie's leg.

"Gracey, come back here." Holding Lily's leash, she took off in pursuit. The hairs on her neck stood as Gracey's excited bark turned into a low keening. She ran down the sidewalk, stopping at the front yard two houses down.

The normally happy dog stood in the driveway, ears flattened against her head, tail tucked between her legs. That other worldly sound came from deep in her throat. She approached her dog, talking to her in a soothing voice. When she reached Gracey, she scooped her up in her arms. "What's the matter, girl?"

Gracey gave her a lick on her chin before tucking her head into Addie's chest. Her heart raced. The feeling of panic from her dream seeped into her bones. The garage door was partially opened, maybe three feet off the ground. A car sat in the driveway. The for-sale sign still sat in the lawn next to her. As far as she knew, no one lived there.

She walked back to her own car, carrying Gracey. The dog clung to her like glue. Lily trotted alongside on her leash, looking back over her shoulder at the house every few feet. Addie turned her car on and set the air conditioning to low. She opened the back hatch and motioned for Lily to jump in. She set Gracey in the car, then gave each a pat on the head. "I'll be right back girls." She shut the hatch.

She walked back to the other house. Each step was like lifting concrete. She glanced up and down her street. Empty. Most were already at work. Reaching the driveway, she skirted the car and approached the garage door.

"Hello?" She waited but didn't get any response. *Of course not. That would be too easy.*

She took a deep breath and continued to the garage. She looked under the door. Only shadows greeted her. The sunshine on her hair and skin did nothing to combat the icy fingers running down her spine.

"Is anyone there?" she tried again. No answer. Bending down for a better look, she gasped at the sneaker clad feet she saw. Whoever was attached to them was lying still on the floor. Too still. She started at frantic barking from her car. Both dogs jumped up against the side window, barking and howling.

She didn't know what to do. But concern for whoever lay on the floor won out. Addie scooted under the garage door and approached the body. A coppery smell reached her nose. "Hey. Are you okay? I'm, uh, Addie Foster. I live up the street."

No answer. No movement. Her head pounded. The headache she had awoken with grew with a vengeance. The bit of sunlight creeping under the door didn't allow for much visibility. She crept closer. "Now would be a good time to wake up and say something."

But as she reached the body on the floor, Addie realized no one would be answering her. Blank, sightless eyes stared straight up. Her feet slid in a liquid on the floor. She scrambled for balance, only to feel herself falling. She threw out her hands to break her fall, landing in a half-crouch, half-kneeling position. Right next to the body. The concrete floor bit into her hands.

She stood on shaky legs and backed away, unable to take her eyes from the dead body. She only stopped when the garage door met her back. Ducking underneath, she escaped into the daylight. And screamed. Blood covered her shoes and pants. Her breath caught in her lungs. Her empty stomach revolted. Acid and bile threatened.

She wiped her hands on her pants, desperate to remove the blood from them. She pulled her phone from her pocket, hitting the first preset.

"I hope you're calling from the parking lot with my drink, young lady."

"Gr-gr-grey. Help me."

"Addie? What's wrong? Where are you?"

"S-s-send help."

"Addie! You're not making any sense. Where are you?"

"I'm at my house. There's a lot of blood. Too much bl-bl-blood. Call the police." The world began to tilt on its axis. She took a few steps towards the grass when her vision dulled at the edges. Then everything faded to black.

Chapter Two

"Ma'am, can you hear me?" The unfamiliar, male voice sounded as though it came from the bottom of a well.

"Ma'am? Open your eyes." More distinct now, the voice grew impatient. Or maybe concerned.

"Ma'am?" she responded. Sheesh. She wasn't *that* old. She opened her eyes, squinting into the bright sunlight. She sat up, maybe a bit quick, and wished she hadn't. The world spun around her, and Addie closed her eyes to stop the motion. Her stomach lurched. She pressed a hand into it.

"You shouldn't try to get up yet," came the same disembodied voice.

"Now you mention that," she grumbled. "And I know this is North Carolina, but I'm not that old." The sound of a chuckle being not so convincingly covered by a cough followed. Then the rustle of clothing. She cracked one eye to see a wall of male crouch in front of her.

"I'm with the police. If you tell me your name, I can call you something other than ma'am."

Yep, there was a hint of amusement at the end of that. She opened both eyes. And stared into dark eyes framed by a craggy face. He may not be GQ cover worthy, but he merited a second look. One brow, dissected by a scar, drew her eye. Brown hair, the color of sinfully dark chocolate, lay close cropped to his skull. The sunlight brought a hammer to the inside of her skull. She closed her eyes again. Her hand shook as she pressed it to her forehead. "Adelaide Foster, or Addie, Officer."

"It's Detective, actually. Detective Jonah Wolfe. There's an ambulance on the way, Ms. Foster."

"I don't need an ambulance."

"You're covered in blood, but I can't see where it's coming from. Can you tell me what happened?"

And it all came flooding back to her. The open garage door. The too still body. The large pool of blood. Her stomach clenched and then rolled. Tears poured down her face. "That poor man. I tr-tr-tried to help him."

"Now, Ms. Foster, uh, calm down. Take a breath. Tell me everything you remember."

"Addie! Addie? Where are you?" Grey's voice echoed down the street, the most welcome sound ever. Even if it blared inside her skull.

"Over here, Grey." She shouldn't have yelled. "Oooh," she muttered into her hands as she covered her face.

"Addie, where are you?" His voice drew closer.

She waved one hand around the corner of the car parked in the driveway. Even that small motion caused her stomach to lurch wildly. "I don't feel so good."

Strong hands grabbed her around the shoulders and lowered her to the ground. "It's best if you lay down until the ambulance gets here." His voice had both softened and roughened. If she weren't so sick, she might have wondered at the zing of sensation racing across her body at the touch of his hands.

"Addie, oh my God, what happened? You can't say things like 'blood' and 'police', then hang up. Girl, you took ten years right off the top."

"Sir, this is a crime scene. I'm going to have to ask you to step back."

"You can ask all you want, but that's my Addie lying there."

The distant wail of an arriving ambulance competed with the voices of the detective and her BFF. It was all too much with the incessant pounding of her head. She welcomed the darkness sliding over her.

*****

A soft beeping dragged her from sleep. Addie cracked one eye, relieved at the sight of Grey asleep in the uncomfortable looking chair next to her. She opened both eyes. The relative dimness of the room told her some time had passed. She tried to sit up but stopped when the cymbals in her head returned. *Note to self: don't do that again.* Grey stirred in the chair.

"Hey, welcome back," he whispered. He rose from the chair in one fluid movement and leaned down to kiss her softly on one hand. "I'd kiss your cheek, but you've been muttering about your head."

"What time is it? Where am I?"

"You're in the hospital. Observation only because you passed out. Twice." He pulled back a perfectly pressed cuff to glance at the gold watch on his wrist. "And it's just past eight. In the evening in case you wondered." He held up a hand when she started to speak. "And before you panic, the girls are with the Aunties."

"Oh, thank you. I haven't seen them since I put them in the car in my driveway." Tears formed on her dark lashes. "If anything happened to them…"

"They're okay, Addie. Doing great actually, since the Aunties are showering them with praise and treats equally." He grimaced. "Can't say the same for the interior of your car. Sorry, but the girls got a bit frantic."

She settled her head back against the pillows, trying to find a spot that didn't hurt. Another thing to worry about. "Oh well, it's only a car. They must have been terrified."

Grey hit the nurse call button. "The night shift nurse came by before you awoke. She said to ring if you needed anything." He gestured with the call light, pointing towards her head. "You need something for the pain."

"No, I'm fine," she protested, but it ended in more grimacing.

A soft knock on the door caught his attention. "See, she's here already. Come in."

But it wasn't a nurse, unless they were wearing suits these days. And a scowl. Over six feet of solid male entered her room. "Ms. Foster, I'm Detective Wolfe. We met this morning. Are you feeling any better? I need to ask you some questions."

Grey stood, forming a barrier between her and the visitor. "Addie is still under the weather, Detective. Might I suggest coming back tomorrow? And calling first?" He did the human equivalent of baring his teeth. And if he had hackles, he would have raised them.

Seemingly not impressed, he stepped further into the room. "You've had a tough day, and I'm sorry for that. But time is critical in a murder investigation. I just need five minutes." Pulling a chair to the opposite side of her bed, he sat and extracted a small notebook from his pocket. "Let's start with this morning. Did anything unusual happen?"

"You mean other than finding a dead body, Detective Wolfe?"

He had the grace to lower his gaze. "Of course, ma'am. I mean Ms. Foster. We know how much you don't like ma'am. I meant leading up to finding the dead body."

She raised her head, turning it slowly to face him. And gasped. Eyes so dark they were almost black stared at her from a chiseled face with more than a hint of five o'clock shadow. The planes of his face were a bit too harsh to be considered classically handsome, but wow. Just wow. She remembered the scar dissecting one eyebrow. She'd have to ask him about that.

"I'm surprised you remembered. What with the dead body and all." She raised a hand to her temple, tried to soothe the pounding within.

Another knock sounded, followed by a tiny blonde woman. "Hi, ma'am. I'm Karen, and I'm your nurse until morning. What can I get for you?"

"Hello, Karen. I'm Greyson, but you can call me Grey. Addie has a terrible headache. And this officer isn't making that any better. Can you bring her something please?"

She watched as Grey bestowed his should be patented megawatt smile on the poor, unsuspecting nurse. Sure enough, the young woman's cheeks pinked up. It never failed. What a shame he was gay.

"Of course, Grey," she murmured to him. "I'd be happy to get her something for pain." And then, almost as if remembering Addie was in the room, she turned to her. "Can you rate your pain on a scale of zero to ten, with ten being the worst pain ever?"

"Oh, I'd give it a five." That earned her a glare from Grey. "Okay, it's more of a seven. But I don't want to be a bother."

Grey patted Addie's hand. "Nonsense, honey, Karen here needs to know how much pain you really have. Don't you, Karen?"

She watched as the smile slid from the other woman's face. Poor thing. More hopes dashed upon the rocks of reality, even if the reality wasn't what she thought. The result was the same.

"Of course. I'll be right back with something for the pain." The petite nurse flounced from the room.

Addie sighed and closed her eyes. "Grey, was that necessary?"

"Yes, it was. Now you'll get pain meds. Hopefully something good."

She heard her other visitor shift in his chair. Her eyes popped back open. "Oh, I forgot you were still here." She felt heat rise across her cheeks. "What I meant was…"

"I know what you meant." He opened his notebook. The scowl on his face deepened.

"You had some questions for me? I'll do my best. The whole thing is a big blur in my mind."

Grey came around the other side of her bed and perched on the end of it, hovering. "Are you sure, darling? You've had a tough day." He rested a hand on her blanket covered leg.

She would have laughed if it wouldn't hurt so much. "I'm sure, pookie." She turned her gaze to the detective. "I'll do my best."

He pulled a pen from his suit coat pocket. "Why don't we start by you telling me what you do remember?"

She tore her eyes away from his and closed them. Resting her head against the pillow, she told him everything she could remember, leaving out the part about the dreams. Surely, he didn't need to know that.

"And where do you work?"

"She owns Smiling Dog Books in town. You must have seen it. On Magnolia Lane, two blocks off the square."

"Sure, next to the coffee shop. Weren't you a little late leaving your house?"

Grey started to say something, but she interrupted. And opened her eyes. "If I was a suspicious person, Officer, I'd think you were accusing me of something."

He didn't blink. "It's Detective, and you *were* the first person to find the body, ma'am."

Well played. Not that she'd be telling him. "I was at the store late last night. Doing inventory." She grimaced. "Not my favorite part of owning a bookstore. Anyway, I went to bed late, so Grey opened this morning."

He looked from one to the other. "So, you two work together as well?"

"As well as what, Detective?"

He raised one brow, the one with the scar, but didn't take the bait. "So, you were leaving for work later than normal. And you happened to notice the open garage door?"

"No, Gracey noticed that."

"Gracey?" He flipped back a few pages, the frown deepening. "Who's Gracey?

"Some detective," Grey muttered, mostly under his breath, earning himself a glare.

"Gracey and Lily are my dogs. They go to work with me. Anyway, Gracey took off running before I could get them in the car. By the time I caught up to her, she was standing on the sidewalk in front of that house, staring. I told you what happened after that."

"Do you remember hearing anything else that morning? Before you left for work?"

Karen entered the room, saving her from answering. "Here you go. I have your medication." She scanned Addie's bracelet and then the pill. "This may make you sleepy as well, so don't get up to use the bathroom without calling for help. Can't have you falling again."

She made the sign of a cross by her heart. "I promise." She swallowed the pill with a sip of water. Then laid back against the pillow. And covered a yawn.

Grey moved closer on the bed. "And that's your cue, Detective."

She tried to not laugh at his obvious protectiveness. "You're not wrong. Could we pick this up tomorrow? Hopefully, I'll be home by then. I can stop by the police station."

"Or I can come to you." He stood, looking down at her as he placed his pen and notebook back in his coat pocket. He pulled a card, handing it to her. She took it, careful not to touch his fingers. His voice alone was enough to handle.

"If you think of anything in the meantime, call me. Anytime." He held her gaze for a moment before leaving the room.

Grey watched him go. Fanning himself, he turned back to her. "Good Lord, if only he didn't play for the wrong team."

She smiled at her best friend. "How can you be so sure?"

"Oh, I know. Besides, think of the pretty babies y'all would make."

She laughed this time, clutching her head. "You are too much, Grey. The man thinks I murdered someone. The last thing he wants to do is have babies with me. Not that I want that either," she rushed to add.

He tilted his blond head. "Tick, tock, Miss Addie. Those eggs of yours aren't getting any younger."

She pulled the coves up around her further. "Nice. Thanks for reminding me. No need to worry, I've resigned myself to only having fur babies. The girls are enough for me." The wistful note in her voice said otherwise.

He stood. After patting her hand, he grabbed his keys. "On that note, I'm going to head home. But I'm only fifteen minutes and a phone call away. Call me if you need anything. I'll swing by your place and grab some clothes for you to go home in tomorrow." He waved a hand over her. "I know you don't want to be seen wearing *that*."

Her eyes drifted shut. "Thank you so much, Grey, for everything."

"Of course, honey. Now get some rest. And no bad dreams tonight."

Chapter Three

Grey pulled his Jeep next to her SUV in the driveway. He switched it off and turned to look at her. "No dreams last night?"

She smiled. "Nope. You must have scared them off."

"More likely, the medication knocked you on your ass. You never take anything stronger than an aspirin."

"That may be it. And now I remember why. Even hours later, I feel a bit fuzzy." She laid a hand on his arm. "I appreciate the ride home." Addie opened the passenger door. Then remembered she didn't have her keys. He came around the hood, holding them up. "I've got you covered. Let me help you."

She turned, groaning as she slid out of the car. Standing on shaky legs, she waited for him to reach her. She placed her arm through his, leaning on him a bit. Her head throbbed, reminding her of what she had endured. She glanced at the yellow police tape blowing in the breeze down the street and shuddered. She'd take the headache over that poor man's fate.

They walked up the driveway and onto the front porch. "Have you heard anything about the murder? Like who he is? Was?"

Grey opened the storm door and slid a key into the lock. "His name was Richard Allen, and he was fifty-one. That's all I know. Maybe Detective Hottie can tell you more."

"Funny. He still thinks I killed that poor man." That thought sent a chill down her spine. But the cacophony of barking from inside banished it.

"My girls!"

"I stopped by and grabbed them from the Aunties this morning. Knew you'd want to see them. And by the sounds of it, they missed you too." He opened the door, and out flew a whirl of fur and prancing feet.

She sat in a porch chair, hands outstretched. The dogs whined and swamped her, licking every inch they could reach. "Hi, Gracey. Hi, Lily." She leaned down, hugging their little furry bodies. "I sure missed you guys last night. Did Aunt Beatrice and Aunt Clementine take good care of you?" she crooned to them.

"Let's get you inside. The reunion can continue there." He shook his head. "You'd think you were gone for a month, not barely a day."

She stood, taking care to not step on little doggy feet. "And that's why I like dogs more than most people I've met."

"Present company excluded, of course."

"Most days." She grabbed the arm of the chair. The porch swayed around her. The girls whined at her feet.

He rushed to her side, swinging her up in his arms. "That's enough for today. Let's get you inside."

"Is this a bad time?"

Grey turned, Addie still in his arms. She clutched her head. "No sudden movements," she cried.

"It's not a great time," Grey answered, carrying her inside. He walked straight to the couch and lowered her to it. "I'm getting you some tea."

"I guess you're not feeling better."

"Now we know why he's a detective," muttered Grey on his way to the kitchen.

"I've had better days." *Crikey!* Why must she be a mess every time she saw him?

"So, we have a name and age." He blew out a breath. "And that's about it. Except for this." He held up a clear evidence bag.

The less than tasty hospital food she'd eaten for breakfast threatened to come back up. She pressed a hand to her stomach. Her distinctive business card, with a smiling Sheltie face on it, stared back at her. "That's mine," she admitted in a small, shaky voice.

"Yes, I know. Detective and all. The better question is, what was he doing with it?"

"I have no idea." A flash of the dreams came to her. Her heart pounded. Her vision grayed. Were her crazy, dark dreams somehow related to this murder? How? Why?

"Can you let me in on whatever has you thinking so hard? I can hear it over here."

No way was she telling him about the dreams. "I, uh, have no idea how he got my card. But I have them in the shop. Maybe he came by and grabbed one."

"Did you recognize him at all?"

She shook her head and immediately regretted it. "I only saw his face for a second. And all that blood." She closed her eyes, but the image of the dead man flashed in her mind. They popped back open.

He pulled his cell from his pocket. "If you think you can handle it, I have a picture I want you to look at. It's just his face. No blood."

Grey walked back in, carrying her tea. "Here you go, sweetie." He placed it on the coffee table in front of her. "Better give it a moment to cool. What's going on in here? I hope you're not upsetting her."

"It's fine. The detective was about to show me a picture of the dead man." She pointed to the evidence bag lying on the table. "He had my card."

"What? Why?"

"That's what I want to know," answered Detective Wolfe in a serious tone.

"You can't really believe Addie had anything to do with this?"

"So far, I have one dead guy, found two houses away from here. She happened to find him. He was carrying her card. What would you think?"

Grey straightened, leaned forward as he spoke. "I'd think you have a bunch of circumstantial evidence."

The detective smirked. "Watched a lot of Law and Order, have you?" He turned to Addie. "Are you ready to look at the picture?"

She nodded, as ready as she'd ever be. She clasped moist palms together. "Ready."

He hit a button his phone and turned it towards her. The picture showed a man lying on what had to be an autopsy table. She, too, watched a lot of police shows. A white sheet covered him to his neck so that only his face and head showed. Death had leeched all color from his face. And yet, it seemed familiar.

She turned to Grey. "Doesn't he look like that creep from the other day?"

"What creep?" asked the detective.

He nodded. "Yeah, that douchebag who gave you a hard time."

Detective Wolfe sat forward in his chair. "What douchebag?"

"A few days ago, this guy, maybe, came in the store."

"He had an attitude from the minute he walked in."

"Do you mind letting Ms. Foster answer the questions? I'll have others for you later."

Grey narrowed his eyes. "My bad."

Addie reached for her tea, more to feel the warmth of the mug than to drink it. "Two days ago, he came in around lunchtime. I remember because I was alone in the store at the time. Grey had stepped out to grab something for us to eat."

"Oh, right, the fabulous pulled pork sandwiches from that new place." He stopped talking at a look from the detective. "Sorry."

She covered Grey's hand with hers. "Anyway, I remember being alone in the store with him. And not feeling very comfortable about that fact. Which is odd, because I'm alone with customers all the time."

"What about him made you feel uncomfortable? Did he do something? Say something?"

"It wasn't anything obvious. He asked me about a recent bestseller. A spy thriller. Which was odd."

"Why?"

"Because he was standing maybe two feet from a display table with over twenty copies of that book on it."

"Oh."

"And then there were his eyes."

"His eyes?"

"Yes. They were cold. Kind of dead. Like there wasn't much behind them, if you know what I mean."

"And his mouth was cruel," Grey added.

The detective scratched his head. "So, you're telling me he had dead eyes and a cruel mouth? That's all?" He glanced at Grey. "I thought you were out getting lunch."

"Don't get your panties in a twist. I arrived back with our lunches as they were talking."

"Huh. I don't suppose he used a credit card."

"For what?"

He released a big breath. "For the spy thriller?"

"Oh. He didn't buy it."

"I scared him off," Grey stated and squeezed her hand.

The detective tilted his head, looked at Grey. "Really?"

"He did. The guy left as soon as Grey came in with lunch."

"Is there anything else you can remember? Anything at all, even if you don't think it's significant."

"He had an accent, but it was very faint. Almost like he didn't want me to know that. And he stared at me in a strange way. That's what made me so uncomfortable." She shuddered at the memory of those cold, dead eyes. "And he made up the story about looking for that book."

"How do you know?"

"He was very vague, asking for that 'latest big book.' He didn't know the title or author. But when I pointed to the table next to him, he nodded."

"Okay. And what about his stare? How was it strange?"

Grey squeezed her hand in silent support. She watched the detective's mouth tighten, ever so slightly. If she hadn't been looking at him, she would have missed it. "He, uh, said all the right things, but he stared at me, like one might a bug under a microscope. It was like he was looking inside of me." She laughed. "I know you think I'm being fanciful. There was just something about him that gave me the creeps. I didn't care that he left without buying the book. I was happy to see him go."

He jotted a few things before glancing at Grey. "You got the same feeling?"

"I almost asked him to leave, but he did so without prompting. Abruptly too."

"Yes, that's right. One second, he was staring at me, then he turned on his heel and left. Never even said goodbye."

"And you never saw him again?"

"No, thank goodness. Well, at least not until the garage yesterday morning."

"The car in the driveway was rented to a Richard Allen at the Wilmington Airport five days ago."

She looked at his expression. Pretty much blank. Yet he was holding something back. *Hmmm.* "You said 'a Richard Allen', as though they were two different people." She tilted her head, never breaking eye contact. And watched the emotions flash across his face. Then his expression closed again.

He stood. "That's all I have for now. Thank you for your time. I'll see myself out."

Grey stood as well. "Hold on. What does this mean? Is Addie in danger?"

"Why would she be in danger? She had an encounter, for lack of a better word, with a man that left her feeling uncomfortable. And now he's dead."

"Wait a minute. How did I become the bad guy here?" She stood up, leveling the playing field. And grabbed the edge of the cough. Okay, maybe not quite equal. "I didn't do anything wrong, Detective. Am I a suspect?"

"Not per se. But you are my only connection to the victim. I'll be in touch." He left her house.

Addie and Grey both watched him go. When the front door closed, she sat back down. "Well, that was interesting."

"I'll say. Did you see the way he watched you? It's really a shame he's straight."

"Grey!" She tossed a throw pillow at him. "What's wrong with you? Someone, some creepy guy, was murdered right down the street. And now I'm connected to it. And he's looking at me, trying to figure out if I am a murderer."

"On TV, they take you in if they really think you killed someone."

"Well, this is real life, not a TV drama. Who knows what they do?" She picked up her tea, taking a sip. And thought back to the discussion of the rental car. Something about how he said it nagged her. It was almost like he didn't think the guy in the garage was Richard Allen.

She realized Grey was staring at her. "What?"

"You tell me." He waved a hand at her. "You have that trying to figure it out face on. What gives?"

"Not sure. Didn't you find it weird the way he said 'a Richard Allen' rented the car? As if the man in the garage wasn't really Richard Allen."

"Not really. They released the victim's name as Richard Allen. Why would they do that if it wasn't him?"

"You're probably right." She yawned, trying to cover it with her hand. "I think I'm going to take a nap right here." She pulled her legs up onto the couch while he tucked her under an old afghan her mother had made.

"Are you going to be alright for a bit? I thought I'd go check in at the store and run some errands."

"I'm fine, just tired. Tell Erin thank you for holding down the fort." The young woman studied English at the University of North Carolina in Wilmington. She'd wandered in one day, the two had hit it off, and Addie hired her on the spot. And never looked back.

He leaned down, kissing her forehead. "Call me if you need anything." Then he pet the girls on their heads. "Take care of your Mommy while I'm gone."

Gracey and Lily turned around a few times and settled on the floor beside her. Ever the watchdogs. They had no idea they were each about seventeen pounds of fluff. "Good girls." She patted both of their heads.

She tucked the afghan up around her face, breathing in the scent of old cotton. Sometimes, she believed she could smell her mother's perfume. Julia Foster had always worn lilac. She joked it was her signature scent. Tears pricked her eyes. Her mother had been gone a long time, but sometimes the loss felt fresh.

She drifted to sleep, but it wasn't a peaceful one. The same faceless man threatened her, his hands reaching for her, seeming to stretch to grab her. For the first time, another man appeared. She was only dimly aware of him, in the shadows at the edge of her dream. He stood very still, as if watching the drama unfold before him.

She turned to run, her heart pounded. But darkness surrounded her. And then, the scary man spoke, a whisper really. *Adelaide.* That's all he said. She woke with a start, sitting up so quickly that her head spun. As she waited for the room to still, she thought about the dream. The bad man had never spoken before. She grabbed her phone off the low coffee table. Late afternoon already.

Grey answered on the first ring. "Addie? Are you okay? I'm on my way back. I grabbed some stuff for dinner. Now don't go getting any ideas. This is a one off."

"He's the man from the store. The one in my dreams. What does this mean?"

"Wait. What? What man? What are you talking about?"

"The man in my dream, the one who's been appearing for over a week now. It's the guy from the garage. Richard Allen. They have the same voice."

"I'm right down the block. Give me a minute. I have to hear this in person." He disconnected.

Addie went into the kitchen to make more tea. Or maybe hot chocolate. That was a favorite of the Aunties. Of course, theirs was laced with something a bit stronger than marshmallows. Although her head scan had been clear, it might be better to wait on the good stuff.

She jumped at a knock on the back slider. Grey always came in through the back. She hadn't heard his car pull up. She pressed a hand to her chest and let him in. "Do not do that! Ten years, right off the top." And then she hugged him. "On the other hand, thank goodness you're here."

He hugged her back and looked over her shoulder at the stove. "Can I hope that's the Aunties version of hot chocolate?"

"For you, it can be. I'll pass."

"I thought they ruled out another head injury."

She pulled a face. "They did. Thank goodness. That concussion protocol sucked. No Internet. No reading! I'm not sure how I survived."

"You really weren't fun to live with."

"Thanks a lot."

"Just keeping it real. But I still don't understand. That was three months ago. Why can't you have a hot toddy now?"

She poured the mixture into two mugs. The scent of warmed chocolate teased her nose. She reached into a cabinet for a bottle of Kahlua, giving his drink a healthy dose. "I probably could. But I'm still feeling off. Probably not a good idea."

They took seats at the table. "Mmmm," Grey moaned after taking his first drink. "Delish. I can't imagine how this is a bad idea." As if to prove his point, he took another sip.

Addie played with her mug, dunking the tiny marshmallows with her spoon. "I have to ask you something."

"Yes, I do think you should jump the hot detective." He grinned in a way that would make the Cheshire Cat proud.

"This is serious, Grey. I need you to be honest with me."

He put down his mug and took her hands in his. "Sorry. You have my full attention."

"Do you think I'm going crazy?" She expected him to laugh. Or snort. But he did neither.

"No," he answered without hesitation.

"Okay, good. But I should have asked this next question first." She leaned toward him and took a big breath, letting it out slowly. "Do you think the dreams are in any way tied to my head injury?" She waited for his equally quick denial.

"Maybe."

"Oh." It was something that had bothered her ever since the nightmares began. She'd never been one to remember her dreams. They were vague and long forgotten by the time she awoke. Not anymore.

"I don't really know, Addie. So maybe is the best I can do. Tell me about this latest one."

She relayed the details. "The voice was the same. But I don't know if that's because we discussed him with the detective. And he's dead now anyway. Richard Allen is dead."

He raised one blond brow before taking a sip. "You don't sound convinced."

"You heard him that day. He had the faintest trace of an accent. Something vaguely Eastern European. I don't think Richard Allen would have one. Do you?"

"Doubtful."

"And why does he have a voice in my dreams now? He's dead." Wind kicked up outside, rattling the kitchen windows. Just what she needed.

"Sounds like we're getting another storm. Look, I don't have any answers. And neither do you. Why don't I make you that dinner? We can watch a movie afterwards. Your choice. And I'm sleeping in the guest room tonight. No argument!"

Love for him clogged her throat. "Sounds like a plan. I'm going to take a shower while you cook." She plucked at her shirt. "I smell like hospital."

He wrinkled his nose. "Well, I wasn't going to tell you. Can't kick a girl when she's down."

"Funny."

Chapter Four

A loud knocking on the front door awoke her from a dreamless sleep. At the last minute, she had taken a pain pill before heading to bed. Her whole body still ached from falling, both in the garage and the driveway. The fact that it seemed to block her dreams was a bonus. But that couldn't be her long-term plan.

The girls raced out of her room, yipping. She got up and threw an old, battered robe over her sleep shorts and tank. Grey's voice floated through her small house, followed by the even louder voices of The Aunties. They really needed hearing aids. She swallowed a groan. She loved her great aunts, really, she did. But she wasn't up for them this morning.

She tightened her belt, and her resolve, plastered a smile on her face and left her room. And immediately regretted it.

"Oh, there's our girl," both of her elderly aunts cried as they descended upon her.

She held her breath against the cloud of lavender that engulfed her.

"Why didn't you tell us what happened?" admonished Aunt Clementine.

"You should have checked in, young lady," added Aunt Beatrice, not to be outdone by her sister. They were twins, but

Clementine had the upper hand. By thirteen whole minutes. And eighty-three years later, she had never let Beatrice forget it. 'Young lady' never failed to crack her up. But well into her thirties, she'd take it.

"I didn't want to worry you." She crossed her fingers of one hand behind her back. In all the craziness, she hadn't thought to tell then.

"Well, it's all the talk down at Dyeing for Change." Aunt Clementine sighed and lowered herself into a chair. "You can imagine my embarrassment when I didn't know my own niece was involved in this mess."

And the desire to groan returned. Grey, bless his heart, stepped into the fray. "Now, Clementine, you know Addie didn't wish to worry you. She, we, thought it would be easier to hear about it when it had all blown over. We were really thinking of you, not wanting to scare y'all."

"Oh, well, when you put it like that." She smiled and fluffed her hair helmet. And just like that, the wind was taken out of her sails. He had a knack for handling The Aunties.

Clementine turned to Addie. "Tell me again why you haven't snatched up this nice man, sugar. You're not getting any younger, dear."

"Because he's gay, Aunt Clementine."

"Oh, that can't be true," replied Beatrice before wolfing down half a chocolate muffin in one bite.

"Oh, I don't know about that." Clementine looked Grey up and down. "Are you sure, dear? About the liking boys thing?"

He never batted an eye. "Since Bobby Holmes's sixth grade party, ma'am. Spin the bottle and all that." He shuddered. "That Linda Sue Boyd cured me of ever wanting to kiss a girl again."

"Well, if you're sure." She turned her gaze back to her great niece. "Now, that detective fella we saw on the news sure can't be gay. He's just way too good looking for that. No offense, Grey."

"None taken. I did tell Addie what beautiful children they would have."

Addie kicked him under the table for that, enjoying the yelp he swallowed. "Aunt Clementine, Detective Wolfe hasn't crossed me off his suspect list yet. He can't very well father my children."

"Well, I never," declared Beatrice. "To think that a Foster would commit such a heinous act. I have a mind to tell him what I think of that."

"No! I, uh, mean no, thank you. I can handle him. It's only because the man that was killed had my business card on him." And then she wished the Earth would open and swallow her. Why had she brought that up?

"What?" cried both aunts in unison.

"The paper surely didn't mention that part," added Clementine.

"And that's because they don't know. That fact was not released to the press. So, I would appreciate you keeping it to yourselves." She leaned in. "We wouldn't want Hester down at Dyeing for Change to know. The whole town would hear about it."

And it worked. Both aunts clucked about knowing something their gossip rival didn't.

Grey stood. "Now ladies, Addie needs her rest. Doctor's orders. Let me walk you out to Betsy."

They both kissed her and let themselves be led outside. Betsy was their 1967 Cadillac. Venetian blue and complete with fins. They took better care of that monstrosity than some people did their kids.

Grey walked back in, grinning from ear to ear.

"They pinched your cheeks, didn't they?"

"Never fails to make me feel like I'm eight all over again."

"You don't look a day over eleven," she replied, tongue firmly in cheek.

"And you don't look a day over forty. Didn't you sleep last night?"

"Thanks a lot." Forty was a sore subject for her, being on the wrong side of thirty, creeping closer to thirty-five every day. "I did, but the past few days have taken their toll."

"I'll cover the shop."

She shook her head. "No, that's okay. I haven't been there in a few days. Can't keep expecting Erin to do everything. Besides, I never finished my inventory from the other night. It'll do me good to keep busy. Not think about what's happened."

"True. Well, I'm going to head home and shower. I'll see you a little later." He came around the table to kiss her cheek before leaving.

She glanced down at the girls, glued to her side as always. "Well, girls, ready to go to work today?"

Gracey and Lily yipped in reply, racing around the table.

"All I need is a quick shower to feel human."

Fifty minutes later, Addie walked into her shop. Knowing she owned this, well, her and the First Bank of Ocean Grove, never failed to thrill her. Both aunts read voraciously. The Victorian they shared held quite an assortment of books, both old and new. One day, she'd love to get her hands on some of them.

She unclipped the girls' leashes. Gracey and Lily ran right to Erin behind the counter, good dogs that they were. Another perk of owning your own business. Every day was bring your dog to work day. Her assistant gave each a cookie, which they took to their bed.

Erin came around the counter and hugged her. She then held her at arm's length and looked her up and down. "Don't look any worse for wear."

"Gee, thanks. I feel okay. Just a little sore. How are things here?"

"Not bad for a mid-week morning. I had time to work on the inventory. Got a lot of it done for you."

Her loathing of inventory was legendary here. "You are a doll. Remind me to give you a raise."

"Yes, please." She reached behind the counter and picked up a piece of paper. "I almost forgot. A Detective Wolfe called. Here's his number. He asked that you call him bask ASAP. I sure hope he looks as yummy as he sounds."

"Oh, he does," quipped Grey as he strode into the store. "Go call him back, Addie. And make sure you put him on speaker."

She plucked the slip of paper from Erin's hand. "I'll go call him now. Get it out of the way. And not on speaker." She turned and headed for her office.

"Spoilsport," Grey called to her retreating back.

Her BFF was always on her to 'find someone' while he remained steadfastly single. She wasn't against dating, maybe even having a relationship. But who had time for that? Between the bookstore and making sure her elderly aunts were okay...

She unlocked her office door and entered, shutting it behind her. No need to have this conversation with an audience. Her fingers trembled as she dialed. It wasn't every day she called the police department, she assured herself. That was enough to make one nervous. It has nothing to do with a tall, rugged detective.

She was about to hang up when he answered, slightly winded. "Detective Wolfe."

"Hi, it's Addie, I mean Adelaide Foster. You wanted me? I mean wanted to talk to me?" Her cheeks grew hot as she mentally kicked herself. *Get ahold of yourself.*

"Yes, Ms. Foster. Thanks for getting back to me so quickly. I need to meet with you. As soon as possible. To discuss the case. I can be there in twenty minutes."

"Oh. Here?" She thought about how much Erin and Grey would enjoy that. "I can come to you if it's easier." She passed the police department every day on her way to the shop. "Really, it's no problem."

"That's okay. I'll come to you. Say eleven?"

She glanced at the clock on the wall. That was twenty-nine minutes from now. Well, better to get it over with. "Sure. That works. Do you know where I am?"

"I'm a detective, remember? I can find you. See you at eleven."

She held the phone pressed to her ear for a few moments after he disconnected. Something about him put her on edge, affected her. Just his rough voice over the phone had her nerve endings humming. No use in thinking about that. He still considered her a suspect. Now, what to do about Erin and Grey?

*****

Twenty-five minutes later, and four early, Detective Wolfe strode through the door. His name suited him, she thought as she watched him enter from behind a tall bookshelf. He was long limbed and sure of himself. If only she wasn't his prey. Taking a deep breath, she approached the counter where he stood.

"Detective Wolfe, welcome to Smiling Dog Books. You get an A for punctuality."

"Thank you for agreeing to meet with me again. I appreciate your cooperation."

"I wasn't aware I had a choice."

He grinned, showing way too many teeth to set her nerves to ease. "There are always choices. This is a better one." He glanced around. "Is there somewhere we can talk?"

"Here is fine. I sent my employees to an early lunch. We're alone for the time being. How may I help you?"

He glanced around again, as if to make sure, before pulling two photos from his inside suit pocket. He laid them on the counter. Each depicted a man. "Have you ever seen any of these men?"

She picked up each photo, one at a time, giving it a thorough perusal. Then shook her head. "No, I don't think so."

"You know you haven't, or you don't think so?"

She straightened her spine. "I don't know either of them. Why? Who are they?"

"They're known associates of Viktor Juric. He's an arms dealer from Croatia originally. Not a nice guy. Viktor is, or was, wanted by Interpol."

Her heart thumped in her chest. "And now he's not. Because he's dead. There wasn't any Richard Allen, was there?"

"No. The better question is why a man like Viktor would be after you."

She sat on the stool behind the counter. Hard. "A-A-After me? Me? But why?" She rubbed her hands up and down her arms for warmth in the suddenly chilly room.

"That's a very good question, isn't it?" He stared at her, not blinking. "What can you tell me about that?"

"Look, I've told you everything that I know. I never met him before that day. He didn't give his name or buy anything with a credit card. He left the store, and frankly, I was glad. I don't know why he had my card or came to the store." She stopped, taking a huge breath. "And I'm more than tired of you treating me like a suspect. Now, if you don't mind, I have work to do."

She stood, planning to show him the door when he grabbed her wrist. And electricity zinged up her arm.

"I never meant to upset you, Ms. Foster. Sit down for another minute. Please."

She watched the planes of his face loosen. One corner of his mouth lifted, revealing a dimple. His dark eyes looked a bit less glacier. So, she sat. He let go of her wrist, and she missed his touch.

"Had no idea you were so, uh, feisty."

"Well, consider yourself warned."

He glanced around the shop. "Surprised your watchdog isn't here. Guarding you." He smirked on that last bit.

She sat up straighter. "Grey is no such thing. He's my, uh. Well, it's none of your business what he is. But he'll be back soon. So, if you have something else to say, now might be a good time."

He dipped his head, a somewhat old-fashioned gesture. "Very well." He gestured to the photos still lying face up on the counter. "Each of his associates is equally dangerous. Arms, terrorism, money laundering, drugs. You name it. I doubt he's here alone. You're sure you've never seen any of them?"

She looked again, giving each a few moments to be sure. "I promise you I have not." She looked up, right into his eyes. "Look, Detective, I would tell you if I knew anything. But I have a small life in a small town. Ocean Grove, North Carolina, isn't exactly the center of international intrigue."

"Agreed. Which makes figuring out why Viktor was here more important. Why was he looking for you? I must warn you.

Once the feds get wind of him showing up here dead, they'll be all over this place."

The muscle quivering in his jaw told her how he felt about that. She had the oddest notion to kiss it. She shook her head to get rid of those thoughts. "I don't know what they think they'll find."

"They don't care about Ocean Grove. Or you. All they want are his associates." He leaned across the counter until his face loomed inches from hers. "And that means using you as bait if necessary."

"Well, then, it's a good thing I have a guard dog, isn't it?" Direct hit, if the scowl on his face meant anything. If only she didn't have to clasp her hands in her lap to keep them from trembling.

"This isn't a game, Ms. Foster. There's no telling what these men are capable of." He slammed down a hand near the pictures.

"That's enough." The tinkle of the bell over the door prevented her from saying anything else.

Grey strode in, oblivious to the tension in the room. He held up a to go bag from Battalion Bar B Que, named for the former firefighters who owned it. "Lunch. And before you say anything, you need to eat, Addie." Erin followed behind him, carrying drinks. "Sorry, Detective, I only brought enough for three. Maybe next time." His tight smile said otherwise.

"No worries, I was leaving." He turned back to her. "Remember what I said. I'll leave these here in case you happen to remember something." He walked out without so much as a goodbye.

"If ever there was a man who needed to get some," Grey joked. "So, what was it this time?"

"Let's eat. I'll tell you over lunch." They carried lunch to a low table with several chairs arranged around it. She liked to encourage readers to come and stay a while. They bought more books that way.

She held the pictures aloft before passing them to Grey. "So, under the heading of bizarre things that can only happen to me, these are international criminals wanted for horrific crimes. Their friend, and leader, was Richard Allen. Better known as Viktor Juric."

"What?" Grey picked up the pictures, studying each, before passing them to Erin. "I've never seen any of them before. Just Juric."

Erin glanced at them. "Me neither."

"Detective Wolfe thinks I am the reason Viktor was here in Ocean Grove. Have you ever heard such nonsense?"

"Last week, I would have agreed with you."

An invisible fist squeezed her heart. "Grey! How can you say that?"

He placed a hand on her arm. "You have to admit, it's odd that he came here, to the store. I can see why the detective would think that. Not that it makes me like him any better," he mumbled half under his breath.

"Down, boy," she said between laughs. "He called you my 'bodyguard', by the way."

Grey struck a pose. "Good! He'd do well to remember that."

She glanced at Erin, who picked at her sandwich. "I don't know what's going on. But maybe it'd be better if you didn't come in for a few days. Just until this is resolved."

Her employee sagged in her chair. "Thank you, Addie. It's nothing personal. I, uh, don't want to be in the crossfire."

How would she ever take that personally? She laid a hand on Erin's. "It's okay. Besides, don't you have a summer class? You can focus on that. I'm sure this will blow over in a few days." And mentally crossed her fingers.

"Thank you for understanding." She wrapped her lunch back up. "Uh, if you don't mind, I think I'll take off now."

"Of course." She tried to not laugh at her employee almost sprinting for the door.

"Lovely," hissed Grey around a mouthful of pork.

"Be nice. There's no reason for Erin to be caught up in this mess." She turned to her best friend. "That goes double for you."

He put down his sandwich. "You can get that thought right out of your head, Addie. I'm not going anywhere. It's you and me forever, like we pinky promised in first grade." He held up one hand, pinky outstretched.

On a half-sob, half-laugh, she linked her pinky with his. "Not sure what I ever did to deserve a friend like you."

He leaned down and kissed her hand. "Right back at you." He unentangled his hand and sat back. "So, what's your plan?"

"My plan?"

"Nice try. You have a plan, or the beginnings of one. You always do. Sitting around waiting for others to figure this out isn't exactly your style."

"You're right. I can't sit around waiting to see if these hooligans show up on my doorstep. What could they possibly want in Ocean Grove? From me? I'm not that exciting."

"True," he joked. He picked up the pictures again. "I'm sure Viktor is the only one we met."

She got up and walked behind the counter. She looked down at the girls, patting their heads. She slipped them both a sliver of pulled chicken from her sandwich. Each wolfed it down and smiled at her for more.

"Agreed. Let's start with him." She clicked on her Internet browser and typed 'Viktor Juric' into Google. Thousands of hits appeared. "Wow, he was famous. Or infamous." She opened the first article. "Hmmm, just like the detective said; drugs, arms, all the big ones. So, what drew him to Ocean Grove?"

"The better question is, what about you drew him here?"

Chapter Five

The front door opened, sending the bell over it tinkling. "Saved by the bell my dear," Grey chortled and left to greet the customer. Grateful for the reprieve, Addie sat down on the stool and pondered his question. Knowing that Viktor had not only come to Ocean Grove but specifically to *her* bookstore had to mean she was involved. But how? And why?

She read the article and then the next. An hour later, she rubbed at her lower back and then her eyes. She glanced down at the girls, asleep on the bed they shared behind the desk.

Grey meandered over to her. "Okay, tell me everything."

"There's not much to tell. He was a ghost, even before he died. Born in Croatia but left in his late twenties, before the war for independence finished. He fought for Croatia, raised through the military ranks. Then disappeared. That's when his life as an international arms dealer began, but the details are sketchy." She tapped the screen. "I found more than two dozen aliases he used between Viktor Juric and Robert Allen."

"Wow, I thought my life was complicated."

"Your love life is. I didn't find any mention of family or a spouse. And it doesn't look like he ever lived in the states. Yet, he was here in Ocean Grove."

"How about his biological family, you know, parents or siblings?"

"I stopped to give my eyes a rest. There were thousands of hits. It would take days to read through them all."

He stroked his trim goatee. "I bet I know who might have better information."

"Oh, no. I am not going to that man for help. Or information. I'll figure out something."

"That man, huh? Feeling an attraction for the hot detective, are we?"

"I'm not. Are you?" She sighed, knowing Grey would get the truth out of her. He always did. But instead of saying anything, he tilted his head and stared at her, as though trying to read her mind. She stared back. For as long as she could. Which was about thirty seconds.

"Alright, so he's cute. That doesn't change anything."

"Ha! I knew it. And cute doesn't begin to cover it." He pointed a finger in her face. And grinned. "Why do you always think you can keep something from me? You never could. Remember in high school when you had that wicked crush on what's his face, the star quarterback? You tried to keep that from me too." He fanned himself. "As if. I was crushing just as hard."

She felt her face warm. Damn her English ancestors! "Yes, Detective Wolfe is, uh, attractive. And there was that nice zing when he touched me." And wanted to bite her tongue.

"There was a zing? He touched you? Where?"

"In the bookstore," she quipped.

"Funny. Where on your body did he touch you, goofball?"

"He grabbed my wrist when I wanted him to leave about a minute after he got here. I was going to show him the door."

He rested his elbows on the counter and his chin in one hand. "Go on. Don't stop there. Did you ravish him in the romance section?"

"Yes, and I'm already pregnant. It's a boy. Jonah Jr." She blew an errant curl out of her eyes. "Can you be serious for even a second?"

"Sure, but you're the one picking out baby names. And isn't Jonah a bit old-fashioned?"

"I like it. The point is, I can't waltz into his office and ask for help. He already looks at me like he thinks I'm holding back information."

"Well, aren't you?"

"Huh?"

"Oh, then you told him about the dreams?"

"Uh, no. He already thinks I'm somehow involved in this mess. Can you imagine what he'd think if I told him about the dreams and how they may, or may not, be related to a recent head injury?"

"Do we care about what he thinks? I thought we just wanted this thing solved."

She dragged her hands through her short curls. "I want this solved. I want to get back to my life."

"But? There was a but in there."

"Is it so wrong to not want him thinking I'm a freak?"

"Of course not. But this is bad. These guys are not the kind you want to mess with. If he can help us, then he has to know everything."

"I'll think about it. In the meantime, I want to dig a little deeper before I speak with him again." She turned back to the computer. Maybe printing out information would help her to organize her thoughts.

The bell chimed over the door, signaling more customers. "Good timing. I need a break from this anyway." She went out to greet the newcomers.

The rest of the afternoon passed in a blur, as Saturdays tended to. Having a festival in town didn't hurt. Foot traffic was always a welcome bonus. During a slower spot, she'd slipped back to her office to print out information she gathered on Juric.

By closing time, she had a growing mountain of articles but wasn't any closer to understanding anything. That only meant one thing. She sighed, knowing she'd have to go talk with Detective Wolfe. Whether or not she'd tell him about the dreams was another matter. Grabbing an old backpack off the floor, she shoved the papers into it and zipped it up.

Then she went out into the store to help Grey close. Because it was Saturday, she closed the shop at five. She glanced around, happy to see several customers still browsing with fifteen minutes left. She saw him at the register, flirting with a cute guy she'd never seen in the store. She gave him a thumbs up and walked around. Picking up stray books as she went, she couldn't stop the smile spreading across her face. Grey deserved to meet someone nice. Maybe this guy was it. She crossed her fingers.

At five minutes after the hour, she walked the last customer out and locked the door behind her. Flipping the sign to closed, she approached the counter. "Tell me you got his number."

"I did better than that. We're having drinks at The Tipsy Gull tonight. And that might lead to dinner and who knows what." He wiggled his eyebrows, making her laugh. But then the smile slid from his face. "Oh, I can't do that tonight. I have to…"

"Stop right there." She held up a hand. "I do not need a babysitter. The girls and I will go home and lock ourselves in."

"And scare the bejesus out of yourself reading about these criminals. You forget, I know you."

"Better than anyone. I didn't forget." She hugged him hard, thankful as always for his presence in her life. "I'm exhausted. The most taxing thing I have planned for tonight is a long, hot shower and the latest rom com on Netflix." She made a sign over her chest. "Cross my heart."

"Well, if you're sure. He was kinda cute."

"Kinda? He was at least a seven, bordering on eight."

"Good thing I'm a solid nine-point-five."

"At least. Go on, get out of here. I'll be right behind you."

"Won't say no to that." He kissed her cheek and left.

Carrying her purse and backpack, she walked behind the desk and smiled at her dogs, lying on the floor. "Okay girls, let's go home and have dinner." Both sprang up, tongues hanging out. She clipped on their leashes and set the alarm. Once outside, she loaded the girls into the back of her small SUV and got in.

Singing along with Alan Jackson on the short ride home, she tried to clear her head. The things she'd read about Viktor and his henchmen disturbed her. *No thinking about that tonight.* All she wanted to do was eat something, take that shower, and lose herself in a good movie.

When she arrived home, she let the girls into the back yard to do their thing. Rifling through her freezer, she found some frozen ravioli Aunt Clementine made last week. She popped it into the oven, then let the girls in. "All right, girls, who wants to eat?" Her words set off a frantic chorus of yipping and yapping. They danced around her feet as she measured out their evening meal.

"I'm going to take a shower, girls. You be good and guard the place." They didn't look up from their dishes. She walked into her bedroom and stripped off her clothes. After tossing them in the laundry basket, she headed into the attached bathroom. She turned the shower on as hot as she could stand it and turned to wash her face at the sink. Despite efforts to forget about everything for a few minutes, her mind whirled with the implications of the detective's words. There wouldn't be any peace until this was solved.

She stood under the just short of boiling water and let the spray ease her tired body. She still ached a bit from the fall but wouldn't be taking any pain medication tonight. She'd find another way to deal with the dreams. She hummed an old tune her mother sang to her at bedtime and allowed the hot water to melt away her troubles.

And it did. Until the girls streaked into the bathroom, growling low in their throats. She barely had time to process this when the sound of breaking glass echoed through her home. Heart pounding, she turned off the water, leaped out of the shower, and grabbed a towel. She tiptoed out to her bedroom, closing and locking the door with shaking hands. Grabbing her cell from the bedside charger, she ran back into the bathroom, locking that door as well. She turned off the lights and crouched on the cold tile floor. The girls crowded around her, lending support as they leaned their furry little bodies into her.

"It's okay, girls. Mommy's going to call 9-1-1. They'll know what to do." And she did. After what seemed like a lifetime, a woman's voice answered. "9-1-1 what's your emergency?"

"S-s-someone's breaking into my h-h-house. H-h-help me," she whispered through her very dry throat.

"Ma'am, I can't hear you. Did you say there's an intruder?"

The sound of splintering wood reached her. Icy tendrils raced along her skin.

"Yes. I'm locked in the b-b-bathroom with my dogs. Please hurry." The girls continued to growl. She placed the phone before her shoulder and cheek and grabbed each of their collars. "Sshh, now, girls." She couldn't have the intruder hear them.

The operator repeated back her address, which Addie confirmed. "Please hurry, I'm s-s-so scared." She broke off when the bathroom door handle rattled. Tears poured down her face. "They're at th-th-this door." She silently recited all the prayers she learned as a child.

"Ma'am, I'm staying on the phone with you. An officer is very close. Stay as quiet as possible. Don't say anything."

No problem. Anything she might have uttered was lodged in her throat. This was it. She was going to die never knowing why or how she was even involved in this mess.

A loud voice drifted through the door. Then another. They were both male, but she couldn't distinguish the words. Suddenly, a gunshot ripped the air. Followed by a thud against the other side of the bathroom door. Addie grabbed the girls in her arms, burying her face in their fur. She tightened into the smallest ball on the floor she could manage. Her heart beat roared in her ears. She held her breath. Seconds ticked by like hours. *What was happening?* Sweat streamed down her back and face. Her legs burned in this position, but she couldn't have moved if she wanted. She was frozen in place, hugging Gracey and Lily.

And then the gentlest knock sounded on the door. "Ms. Foster? Are you in there? It's Detective Wolfe. You're okay now."

Was this a trick? What was he doing here? Could the intruder have gotten his name somehow? "How do I know it's really you?" she squeaked out. The girls began to whine, licking her face.

"Where's your watch dog? Grey?"

And just like that, she was saved. Addie leapt up, unlocked the door, and launched herself at him. She felt his arms go around her even as he stumbled backwards. "I've got you," he mumbled near her ear. The girls danced around them both, sniffing at the stranger's pantlegs, somehow knowing he was a good guy.

And then she remembered she was wearing a towel. And nothing else.

Chapter Six

For the length of a heartbeat, it didn't matter. She drew in strength from his arms surrounding her. His warm breath ruffling her damp hair. Then she stepped back, pulling the towel firmly around her.

"Oh, um, I'm sorry." Gracey took that moment to play a game and tugged on the edge of her towel. It slid a little lower. "Gracey, no. Bad girl." The crestfallen dog released the material, ears flattened against her head, eyes downcast. She reached down with the hand not gripping the towel to pet her head. "Sorry, girl. I'm a bit rattled."

That's when she noticed the body lying near the doorway. And felt the floor start to tilt.

"No, you don't. I've got you." He reached out, grabbing both of her upper arms. "Stay with me." He shook her slightly. Just enough to grab her attention.

"I'm f-f-fine. Really. You'd think I'd be used to this by now." She kept her gaze straight ahead to avoid seeing the body again.

"Ms. Foster, I have to get you out of here. This is a crime scene."

She shook her head and laughed. A loud, high-pitched, bordering on hysteria laugh. A laugh that wasn't going to end.

"My bedroom is a crime scene." She clamped her lips together and closed her eyes. "I laugh when I'm nervous."

And then he did the most unexpected thing. He chuckled. A deep, hearty chuckle that vibrated up from his chest.

Her eyes sprang open, and she stared right into his dark ones. "Oh."

"After everything you've just been through, no one can blame you for laughing. Or screaming. Or even throwing something. But I'd prefer you not cry. Anything but that."

She took a step back from him and the body on the floor. "I need to get dressed." They were standing in her bathroom. Her room! And she was wearing a towel.

"Of course. I, uh, just need to cordon off this area. Could you maybe grab something and get dressed somewhere else?'

The sounds of more people in the house reached them. "That will be the rest of my department. There's going to be a lot of explaining and paperwork."

"Why?" Then she remembered the body on the floor. "Oh, yes, of course. Could you grab the girls' leashes? They're hanging inside the front door."

He nodded and left the room. She whistled and pointed to her bed. Both dogs jumped up, heads tilted. "Who wants to go for a ride?" Gracey yipped. Lily wagged her tail. She gave them a hand signal to lie down and then to stay. Once they complied, she ripped open a drawer, grabbing the first clothes she reached.

Detective Wolfe walked back in, carrying two leashes. "Here you go."

"Do you mind clipping them on their collars? My hands are full."

He glanced at her hands at the same time she remembered she was holding underwear. Red, lacey underwear. The tips of his ears reddened. "Yes, I can see that." He turned his back to her and approached the dogs. "They won't bite, will they?"

The thought of him being intimidated by two small, shaggy dogs would have made her laugh if the circumstances were different. "Gracey, Lily, Detective Wolfe is a friend."

At the word 'friend', two sets of ears swiveled forward. Two pink tongues lolled. Two noses sniffed his outstretched hand. He gave them a minute to sniff before he clipped on their leashes.

"If you could keep them for a moment, I'll go dress in the guest bath." Clutching the towel and her clothing, she fled from the room without looking at the body again. Shaking her head at how crazy her life had become, Addie dashed into the living room, only to halt at the sight of what must have been the entire Ocean Grove Police Department in her house.

"Oh, uh, excuse me." She walked as quickly as she could into the half bath, securing the door behind her. Throwing on clothing, she glanced in the mirror. Her reflection gave her a fright. Her skin was almost the color of milk, her ebony curls standing out even more than usual. Nothing she could do about that. Dressed in shorts and a T-shirt and barefoot, she left the haven of the bathroom.

Every light in her house blazed. People in uniform and jumpsuits milled about in a seemingly organized chaos. She searched the crowd for a familiar face. But he wasn't anywhere in sight. A female officer approached her. "Ms. Foster? My name is Officer Burke. Could you come with me, please?" The woman looked about sixteen, except for the deadly gun strapped to her hip.

"Of course. Do you know where the detective took my dogs?"

"Yes, ma'am, they're outside waiting for you."

"Oh, good." It might be silly to worry about her dogs after what had happened, but they were family. She followed the woman out her front door. And there was oh so serious Detective Wolfe, sitting in one of her porch chairs, petting the girls.

"Be warned. They shed. A lot." She pointed to several clumps of white and gray hair clinging to his suit pants.

He stood at her approach. "I'll survive. That's what dry cleaners are for." He glanced down at her toes, with their neon orange polish. "You might want shoes."

She glanced down, following his gaze. "Oh. I forgot. Underwear was a higher priority."

He cleared his throat. "Yes, I can see where it might be." He glanced through her front windows. "Is there someone you'd like to call? Or somewhere I can drop you off after I ask some questions."

"Grey! Oh, he's going to beat himself up when he hears about this." She noticed his raised brow. "He offered to come home with me tonight. Again. But I told him I'd be okay."

"So, Grey doesn't live here, then? I got the feeling you two were, uh, together."

"Grey? And me?" She broke off laughing until tears leaked from her eyes. She held her already sore ribs. "Oh, I have to remember to not do that. Why would you think Grey and I were a couple?"

"Oh, I don't know. Maybe because he's always with you and hovers over you like a boyfriend or husband or something." He looked away, mumbling something under his breath.

"Oh, yeah, we get that a lot. Grey is my BFF. My gay BFF at that. He's on a date." She thought about calling him but then remembered his reference to dinner and more. "No, I'll call him tomorrow. Give him the night off guard duty."

"Then is there anyone else I can call for you?"

"Nope. No boyfriend or husband or anything. I'll just head to the Aunties' when I'm done here."

"The Aunties'?"

"My great aunts, Clementine and Beatrice. They live over on Sea Grass Way. I can stay with them until this gets straightened out." She remembered how serious this had become. "On the other hand, maybe a hotel is a better idea. I don't feel right dragging them into this."

"I'm not sure staying in a hotel is the safest way to go."

"Well, staying here wasn't safe. And my aunts are in their eighties. No way am I putting them at risk."

"Detective Wolfe, I need to speak with you." An older man with white hair approached them. "Ms. Foster, I am Chief Winters." He shook her hand. "I'm sorry for your trouble. But I have to ask you to leave until we finish processing the crime scene."

"No problem." She glanced around, shivering. "No need to hurry. I'm not anxious to come back here anytime soon. Could I grab a few things first?"

"I can't really let you back in there." He motioned to Officer Burke. "Ms. Foster is going to need some things for a few days. But I can't let her back in there. Do you mind?"

"Sure, Chief." She pulled Addie a few feet to the side. "Sorry about this. But better me rifling through your stuff than one of the guys, right?"

She smiled for the first time since this whole nightmare began. "Agreed. I hate to be a bother."

The officer waved a hand between them. "Not at all. I'm happy to help."

"If you're sure, then could you grab maybe a few days' worth of clothing. You pick. And I'll need stuff from the bathroom, but I can buy it later. I have suitcases in my bedroom closet."

"I got you covered. Give me a few minutes."

She couldn't help but be aware of Detective Wolfe overhearing the conversation. She tried not to think about being in only a towel earlier. She turned to his boss. "So, Chief Winters, what do I do now?" She smiled at the sight of the chief of police scratching the girls behind their soft ears. "Chief Winters?"

"Oh, sorry. They really are cuties." He straightened up. "Now, we need you to come down to the department to give a statement. There are some other people who'll want to talk with you." The grimace on his face let her know he was referring to the 'feds', as the detective had warned earlier today.

She glanced at the detective, but his face was a mask. No hints there. "Certainly, Chief. Whatever it takes."

"Good. I'll have Officer Burke drive you when she's finished in there."

She had hoped Detective Wolfe would be with her, as he was at least familiar. "If it's all the same, I'll drive my own car. I'm going to need it anyway."

She moved to the other chair and sat, taking the leashes from him. "Thank you for watching the girls for me."

"My pleasure." A ghost of a smile flashed across his face. She couldn't help admiring the five o'clock shadow that darkened his jaw, making him look rugged. Or more rugged. Their eyes held for a moment. And then the chief spoke up.

"Wolfe, you know what we have to do."

"Yes, sir." He gave the dogs one final pat before standing." I have to go."

She watched as the two men walked to a police vehicle and drove away. She wondered what that was about.

"I hope I thought of everything."

She jumped at the voice just behind her. She turned, a hand on her chest. "Sorry. I spook easily these days."

"It's no wonder after what you've been through. I should have announced myself sooner. Sorry. Anyway, I grabbed your phone and charger as well." She grinned. "Can't live without those."

Addie returned the smile. "You're right about that. Thanks for thinking of it."

She handed over a small bag and her purse. "And I grabbed some things for your dogs. Food, bowls, and a few toys."

Tears came to her eyes. "That was very kind, thank you. The girls are freaked out enough by what happened. These will help them adjust to staying in a strange place for a few days."

"I assume you're taking your own car. Let me wheel this suitcase to it, then you can follow me."

They walked to Addie's SUV and waited for someone to move the police car blocking it. "Officer Burke, can you tell me what was going down between the Chief and Detective Wolfe? They both looked grim when they left."

"It's Natalie, please. And that's procedure when there's a shooting. Especially with a fatal one. In this situation, there can't be any doubt that Jonah, I mean Detective Wolfe, is in the clear. But there are hoops he'll have to jump through before he can get his gun back."

"His gun? They'll take his gun? I'd hate to think he's in trouble because of me."

The other woman waved as a young officer moved the car from behind Addie's. "Like I said, it's just procedure. Shouldn't take long to have him back at work." She pointed to a squad car parked in the street. "That's mine. You can follow me."

"Okay, I will." She put the girls and then her bags into her car, mind racing, before sliding into the driver's seat. She drove on auto pilot, following the officer. It gave her time to digest a few things. For saving her life, Detective Wolfe now had to defend himself and his actions to, well, she didn't know whom but to someone. That didn't seem fair. And in a tiny corner of her brain, she wondered about Natalie slipping and calling him by his first name. Did that mean anything? Were they involved? She seemed kind of young for him, but who knew?

She stopped at a red light and looked at the girls in the rear-view mirror. Each lay gnawing on a toy she had thrown in for them. "Hey, girls." Their ears swiveled in her direction. "You'll have to make sure Mommy stays on track. We don't care if Detective Wolfe has a girlfriend, do we?" Since they couldn't answer, she tapped her fingers on the wheel. The last thing she needed to worry about was the man's relationship status.

The light turned green, and she followed her behind the police station to an employee parking lot. Getting out, she grabbed the girls' leashes and walked them over to some grass under a crepe myrtle. She waited as each did their thing, then joined Natalie at the back door.

"Are you sure I can park here?

"Of course. And the dogs are fine, just keep them with you."

"Thanks. I worried about that. Even at night, it's too hot to keep them in the car."

She followed her into the building. Natalie swiped her identification to get them through a locked door. Addie looked around, curious at the scene. She'd never even been to the police department, let alone back here. The labyrinth of desks and several walled off cubicles could have been any office setting. The holding cell in the far corner said otherwise. And sent a shiver down her spine. *How had her life come to this?*

The other woman opened a door. She turned to her, making a face. "Sorry to put you in the interrogation room, but we're a small department, and this at least gives some privacy."

"That's okay. We'll be fine. Thank you for everything." She followed her inside.

"Of course. Someone will be in to speak with you in a moment. Can I get you some water?"

"That'd be great. And maybe a bottle for the girls."

"I'll be right back. Make yourself at home."

Addie waited until she left and then led the dogs to a corner of the room. She motioned for them to stay and gave each a cookie. "Good girls." She looked around the room. She'd have to tell Grey that this looked like any they had seen on a TV cop show. She shivered a bit at that. But at least she wasn't handcuffed to the table.

She'd no sooner sat, when a knock at the door preceded a man and woman in suits entering. The guy approached her, holding out his hand. "Ms. Foster, I'm Agent Williams with the FBI." He shook her hand, then flashed his badge. "And this is my partner, Agent Fisher. We'd like to ask you some questions."

Both agents wore dark suits with matching bland looks on their faces. He motioned for her to take a seat. She did, with them both sitting opposite her.

Another knock announced Natalie's return. The officer walked in and handed her two bottles of water. She glanced at the agents, the smile fading from her face. "I'll see you later, Ms. Foster." She left the room.

Pulling a small bowl from her bag, she filled it with water from one bottle. "Excuse me a moment." Without waiting for their permission, she got up and crossed to her dogs. "Here you go, girls." She placed it in front of them before retaking her seat.

Agent Fischer nodded to the dogs. "They seem well-behaved."

"Yes. I've had them since they were eight weeks old. They're litter mates. But we aren't here to talk about my dogs, no matter how well-behaved they are."

"You prefer the direct approach. Good. That'll save us time." Agent Williams opened a manila folder and took out three pictures, displaying them on the table. He pushed two off to the side. "This was Viktor Juric's right hand man, Goran Vukovik. Nasty piece of work, that one. Your detective should get a commendation for ridding the Earth of him."

Her detective? "I still don't have any idea what this has to do with me. I own a bookstore. In a small town. Before this happened, the most dangerous thing I'd ever done was climb a ladder without a spotter. Well, unless you count a pair of septuagenarians."

"We know all about you, Ms. Foster."

She swallowed hard. "You do?" *Was Big Brother watching?*

Agent Fischer leaned forward. "Once we got this case, we read everything about you we could get our hands on. It wasn't much."

"Ouch."

"What my partner means is, no red flags." He flipped open a small notebook. "Father unknown, mother died when you were seven, raised by one Beatrice Foster and one Clementine Foster, great aunts on your maternal side."

She laughed. Couldn't help it. "Beatrice never gets to go first. She'd like you." She clapped a hand over her mouth, stifling a giggle. "I also get verbal diarrhea when I'm nervous," she muttered through her fingers.

"As I was saying. Good grades in high school, partial scholarship to UNC-Wilmington, graduated magna cum laude with a degree in English, minor in psychology. Moved back to Ocean

Grove afterwards. Opened the Smiling Dog Books in 2010. Not so much as a parking ticket."

"Wow. I really am boring."

"The point is, nothing in your history screams international thugs."

She shook her head.

"And yet, here we are."

"Yes." She clasped her hands together on the table to keep from tapping her fingers. Agent Williams seemed more bothered by her lack of drama than relieved.

"We must be missing something." He looked over his notes. "Do you know anything about your biological father?"

"No. I asked my mom when I was little, but she didn't really answer me. Sort of talked around it. Then she died. I asked my Aunt Clementine when I was in high school. I remember her frowning. She said my mother had met him her senior year of college. She had an internship in Washington, D.C. She came home and graduated before she realized she was pregnant. She never named my father, just said 'he wasn't fatherhood material'. I never asked again."

The two agents exchanged looks but didn't comment. Agent Williams pointed to the pictures. "I know you've already been asked this, but you've never seen the other two men before?"

"No, never, as I told Detective Wolfe."

"Very good. Take us through what happened tonight."

She leaned back in her chair before recounting the events. Other than her hands shaking, she felt calm. Which was odd, since she was almost murdered tonight. She had no doubt of that. If Detective Wolfe hadn't shown up when he did. She shuddered. No, that didn't bear thinking about. When she finished, she took a long drink of water.

"What happens now?"

"We don't know if the third man came with Juric and Vukovic." He tapped the last picture. "Kazimir Maric, Vukovic's cousin. If he is here, he may be bent on finishing whatever it is the other two started."

Tiny hairs stood on the back of her neck. "You m-m-mean kill me, don't you? That's what he came here to do."

He offered a weak smile. "Well, yes. We just don't know why."

She dropped her head into her hands, concentrated on her breathing. In. Out. "Detective Wolfe mentioned you might want to use me as, uh, bait. How would that work?"

The female agent leaned forward, resting her hands on the table. "We would never put you in that kind of danger, Ms. Foster." A look from her partner silenced her.

"What Agent Fischer was trying to say is that of course we will protect you in any way we can. Let's face it, your life isn't going to be your own again until this man is caught. For some unknown reason, they focused on you. He won't stop."

She clutched the edge of the table until the old wood bit into her hands. The look that passed between the agents didn't help. *In. Out. Focus.* She wanted her life back. She wanted everyone in said life to be safe. She sat up, straightening her spine and gathering her courage. "Tell me what I have to do."

Chapter Seven

Addie sat in the middle of the hotel room bed, wrapped in yet another towel, and watched the girls sleep. Gracey and Lily lay spread out on their sides, backs pressed against one another, oblivious to the events of the day. Lucky dogs. Even though midnight had come and gone, she remained wide awake.

She eased off the bed, trying to not disturb the girls. Someone should be getting their rest. Lily cracked one eye, as if to make sure her mistress was okay, then closed it. She grabbed her pajamas and went into the bathroom. Clearing part of the fogged mirror, she peered into it. The dark circles had spread and deepened. But considering she could be dead, she'd take it. She hung up her towel and slipped into underwear and her sleep shorts and an old shirt from college. She started to finger comb her curls when a knock sounded at the door.

She bolted from the bathroom to find the girls standing on the edge of the bed, facing the door. Both barked up a storm. She shushed them with a word and approached it. Looking through the peep hole, she spotted the uniformed officer who had escorted her here earlier. Next to him stood Detective Wolfe.

Addie backed away from the door, took a steadying breath, and opened it. "Gentlemen," she greeted them.

The officer, whose name she had forgotten, cleared his throat. "Uh, sorry to bother you, Ms. Foster. Detective Wolfe asked to speak with you."

"Of course, Officer," she checked his name tag, "Harris. Please, Detective Wolfe, come in."

She stepped back to allow him to pass. And even though his suit was rumpled and tie loosened, he smelled good. Something spicy with a hint of the outdoors and all male. She shut the door behind him, locking it. "I'd offer you something, but I don't have anything other than dog food."

He waved a hand. "No worries. I'm not hungry."

"Ah, you're one of those. Lucky." She noticed the air conditioning had kicked back on. And she didn't sleep in a bra. She crossed her arms and sat at the table.

"One of what?" he asked before taking the other seat.

The girls kept their down position on the bed but had crawled to the very edge, necks outstretched, trying to reach him. Gracey whined while Lily panted.

"People who don't eat when they're nervous. It might be a female thing, but you either eat when stressed or can't eat. Sadly, I fall into the former. I've already raided the vending machine for a Snickers and potato chips. Even though they didn't have my favorite flavor." She shut her eyes for a second. "I'm sorry. Apparently, I don't only laugh when nervous. I babble as well."

"I stopped through a drive thru on the way over, if that helps." He rolled his head on his shoulders. "It's been quite a day." He looked at her as though trying to figure something out. "I'll guess cheddar."

"Cheddar?"

"Your favorite potato chip flavor."

"Oh. Well, you'd be wrong. Sour cream and onion." She drew her bare legs up under her in the chair. "But I'd guess you didn't come to discuss snack food choices."

He pulled at the knot of his tie, loosening it further before sliding it off altogether. Then he stood. "Do you mind if I take off my coat?"

She shook her head.

He slid off the suit coat, folding it and placing it over the back of his chair. His movements were so controlled, precise, that she was ill prepared for what came next.

"Are you crazy?" he exploded before pacing the length of the room. "What could you possibly have been thinking? They don't care about you. You're a means to an end."

"I know," she uttered in a small voice.

"You know? You know???" He dragged a hand through his close-cropped hair. "And yet you've agreed to this harebrained scheme. You must be crazy."

The dogs' ears flattened against their heads at his tone. "It's okay," she murmured to them. She curled up tighter on the chair, trying to make herself smaller, maybe even disappear. "I want my life back."

He stopped at her answer, his shoulders drooping. "But at what cost?"

Tears gathered in the corners of her eyes. She dashed them away with the heels of both hands. "What choice do I have? That man, the one remaining, doesn't care about me or my elderly aunts or Grey. Just by being in my life, they have targets on their backs. What would you have me do?"

"Anything else. Something that doesn't put you in the line of fire." He paced again, slower this time, muttering under his breath.

She stood, walked in front of him, stopped him from his pacing. And laid a hand on his arm. The heat of his flesh burned her through the thin cotton of his dress shirt. "Why, Detective Foster, be careful. It almost seems as though you care about me."

Emotion flared in his eyes. Lust, maybe. With a dash of loneliness. It was gone before she could say for sure. "I care about your safety. I don't want anything to happen to you. They say they'll protect you, but dammit they can't guarantee that."

She dropped her hand and turned away. "Really could use some junk food about now." She walked to the door, hand on the knob. "Thank you for your concern, Detective. Now, if you're done, I need some sleep."

He stared at her for a few moments before picking up his tie and suit coat. And patted each of the dogs on their heads. "'Night, girls." When he reached the door, standing way too close to her, he stopped. "I don't want anything to happen to you." And then he was gone.

Addie murmured goodnight to the officer guarding her and then closed and locked the door. She leaned back against it and closed her eyes. Blew out a deep breath. "Wow, just wow." When she opened her eyes, the girls were looking at her, heads cocked. And she laughed, mostly at herself.

"Your Mommy is silly, girls. No use wasting emotions on a guy like that. I'm just a case to him." She turned off the lights and crawled into bed. She smiled in the dark as the girls each took one side of her, snuggling up against her legs. Her life might be crumbling around her, but at least she had them.

*****

She struggled against the ropes binding her to the chair. But they tightened with her frantic attempts. The course grain bit into her wrists. An acrid taste of smoke burned her nose and throat. A maniacal laugh split the air, taunting her. She was running out of time. She heard the heavy slam of a metal door. He was gone, left her here to die. Even though he said he would, hope had fluttered in her chest. Until now.

She drew in a breath and regretted it as she coughed. She bent her neck, trying to bury her nose into the material of her shirt. No luck there. She held her breath until her lungs burned, forcing her to drag air deep into them. More smoke entered, searing her flesh.

No longer caring about the pain, she pulled again and again at the binds. In a last desperate attempt at escape, she threw her weight to one side, tipping the chair over and falling to the floor. Her head fit the concrete, sending stars around the edges of her vision.

And then, when all hope seemed lost, she heard a faint, masculine voice. "I won't let him hurt you."

She came awake all at once, still struggling to free her arms. And realized it was the weight of two Shelties pinning her in place in the bed. Gracey and Lily, realizing she was awake, pounced on her. She accepted their kisses, glad to be here with them and not in the burning room. Gracey whined, jumped off the bed, and ran to the door.

"Okay, I'll take you out in a minute." She jumped out of bed and dashed into the bathroom to relieve her own bladder. After washing her hands, Addie pulled on sweats and slid her feet into flip flops. She grabbed both leashes and clipped them to the girls' collars. "Okay, let's go." Both yipped and spun in tight circles.

She opened the door to find another officer seated outside of it. He stood up at her approach. "Morning, Ms. Foster. I'm Officer Bradley, or Mike. I'm your day shift person. Going somewhere?"

"Good morning, Mike. And please, call me Addie. The girls here, Gracey and Lily, have to take their morning walk." Both danced at the end of their leashes as if illustrating her point.

"Those are some cute dogs. Kind of look like a Collie I had as a kid. Only smaller."

"I get that a lot. Gracey and Lily are Shetland Sheepdogs. They're full grown. Years and years ago, Collies and other breeds were cross bred with a small native herding dog on the Shetland Islands. That's why they're this size."

The girls paced around, tangling their leashes. "That's my cue. They really have to go."

"Consider me your shadow. Got my orders to not let you out of my sight."

He led the way, checking around the corner and then in the stairwell, before allowing Addie and the girls to proceed. His professionalism impressed her. She felt safe with Mike. Once outside, they walked to a small patch of grass off the parking lot.

"I'm going to grab a soda from the vending machine over there. I'll be back in less than a minute, if you're okay with that."

"Sure, Mike. It's broad daylight out here. What could happen?"

She let the girls off their leads and watched them frolic to and fro, sniffing every blade of grass and playing a game of canine tag with each other. Standing here, with the sun shining on her, watching the dogs play, she could almost forget the craziness of her life. Almost.

Then she remembered the awful dream. Her heart raced. Fear left a bitter taste in her mouth. Each seemed more real than the last, more prophetic. Each had her in more danger than the last. She could still taste the acrid smoke on her tongue, as though she had been in the burning room. She shivered, fear chilling her despite the morning's heat.

She tried to shake off her mood and thought of Grey. They had spoken briefly last night and agreed that he would keep the store open and watch The Aunties for her. She wouldn't risk their lives by coming around until this thing ended. He hadn't liked it one bit. But her insistence that her elderly aunts needed his protection brought him around.

She rubbed at her chest where a funny little ache had developed. She missed her family. Clementine with her bright red bordering on orange hair. Beatrice with her 'old lady blue' rinse, as she called it. And shocking pink lipstick. Both women spent a lot of time at Dyeing for Change, and not only for the gossip. And Grey, who had been through everything with her. The death of her mother, numerous broken hearts, opening her bookstore. They often joked they'd be perfect for each other. If only she was a guy. Maybe when this was done, she'd take him up on his offer to have a child together. Neither of them was getting any younger. Lost in these thoughts, she didn't hear the stranger approach something hard jabbed her in the back.

"Why don't we go for a drive?" His tone, cold as a January night, didn't match his words. He shoved the gun barrel further into her back, letting her know this wasn't a request.

She looked around, trying to find Mike. But he was nowhere in sight. Her pulse thundered in her ears. All round her, it was a normal summer morning. Birds chirped in the trees. A lawn mower sounded in the distance. The normalcy of its roar brought tears to her eyes.

"If you're looking for your officer friend, he can't help you."

"D-d-did you hurt him?" she stammered past the fear clutching her throat.

"Let's just say he'll have one hell of a headache when he wakes up. If he wakes up." He grabbed her arm with his free hand, twisting it. "Enough chatter. Move."

"But my dogs. I can't just leave them here. They could get hit by a car."

"I could put a bullet in their brains if you'd prefer."

Sweat broke out over her entire body, coating her in icy fear. "No, please."

"Then move it." Without another word, he shoved her towards a white panel van parked at the edge of the lot.

Think. She had to find a way out of this mess. If he got her in that van, she was a goner for sure. She'd seen enough true crime on TV to know that. But she didn't have mace or know any fancy karate moves. She'd read once about lacing your keys between your fingers, but they were up in her room. What could she do?

They drew closer to the van. With each leaden step, the idea that she was going to die became her reality. *Do something!* Her eyes darted here and there, desperate to find someone who could help her. But she was alone with the man with a gun.

The van sat close to the vending area. Where Mike had gone? Something shiny and black caught her attention. Looking down, she spied a pair of men's work boots. And there was Mike, lying too still between two parked cars. Her hand flew to her mouth. Blood trickled down the side of his face.

"I told you he wouldn't be able to help you. Now walk to the van. And don't try anything stupid."

If only she had anything stupid to try. She'd settle for that. But her mind became a black hole of fear and dread. She stumbled and would have fallen, but he grabbed her by the arm, dragging her back upright.

"I said no tricks," he hissed.

She made it the last few feet to the van, even though her knees felt like linguine. He motioned with the gun for her to open the side door. When she did, he grabbed a length of rope and bound her hands together behind her back. The bite of it against her flesh brought the dream back to her full force.

She was going to die. Tears began to stream down her face. "Please. I have no idea who you are or what you want with me. I don't deserve this. Please let me go."

He shoved her into the van. She landed on her side, arms behind her, head banging against the metal floor. Her eyes widened as he grabbed more rope and tied her ankles together. He shoved the gun into a holster under his arm. "You are what we call collateral damage." With that cryptic message, he closed the door. She heard him get in the front. Then the rumble of the engine starting. She lost her balance, sliding across the floor when he peeled out of the lot.

Alone in the back of the van, Addie squirmed on the floor, desperate to find a comfortable position. But she couldn't move very much. She looked everywhere in her line of vision. *Surely, there must be something here I can use.* She dismissed that idea as soon as it formed. She wasn't MacGyver.

The windows of the van had been painted black, allowing in very little light. Disoriented from everything that had happened, she had no idea if they drove for ten minutes or an hour. *Do something!* The command ran on an endless loop in her brain, but she lay there helpless.

Too soon, the van came to a halt. She held her breath and strained to hear something. Anything. But other than the driver door opening and slamming, it was silent. Time ticked by as she waited for him to return. Dreaded really. What did he mean by collateral damage? It didn't matter anyway. She was going to die.

Fresh tears leaked from her eyes. Her head ached from connecting with the hard floor.

The man jerked open the side door. Bright sunlight flooded the van, stabbing her eyes. He yanked her into a sitting position, then cut the ropes around her ankles. He pulled her out of the van until she stood on shaking legs, facing him. His face came into view. He was the third man from the pictures she had seen. A known associate of the others. She wished she had a way of letting Detective Wolfe know.

Her captor grabbed her by the arm once again, dragging her towards an old, abandoned building. She turned her head left and right. Recognition dawned. She was in an old industrial park that had sat empty for years. No one would be around to save her. Hope fell away.

"I have money," she blurted to him. "Not a lot, but I'll give you everything I have."

"You Americans," he growled, his accent more pronounced in his disgust. He spat on the ground. "You think money can buy everything. I don't want your money. Money can't bring back my friends. But your death will bring revenge. That's something you can't put a price on."

"What? I don't understand. How do I figure in this? What did I ever do to you?" Her mind raced. Nothing he said made any sense to her. Her head ached, making it hard to think.

"Enough." He jerked her almost off her feet and dragged her to the warehouse. "It is not for you to know."

More vague words that didn't make sense to her. She followed along, trying to keep up with his brisk pace. He let go of her to open the door, flashing his gun to ensure her cooperation. Inside, her eyes adjusted to the dimness. They must have been using this as their base. Three sleeping bags lay open on the floor. Remains of fast food littered the ground. Old, wooden packing crates lay stacked around the perimeter of the room.

He shoved her from behind, causing her to stumble further into the room. That's when she saw it. The chair. The metal chair from her dream. And on the ground next to it sat several gasoline cans.

"P-p-please don't do this," she begged.

He shrugged one shoulder. "Your life means nothing to me. You are a means to an end." He pointed to the sleeping bags. "Their lives meant nothing to you. Snuffed out as though they never existed. Yet, they were my friends, brothers. And now I am the only one left. He must pay."

"He who?" she croaked. Icy chills swept over her. His eyes, the flat, dull eyes of a shark, held no expression. As though nothing lay behind them. She had no trouble believing he would kill her without so much as a second thought. Tears sprang to her eyes.

"It doesn't matter." He grabbed her by the arms, pulling her towards the chair.

She was out of time. Out of desperation, she kicked at his knee, hoping to slow him down. He cursed viciously in a language she didn't understand.

"You will pay for that."

His fist came out of nowhere, smashing into her temple. Stars burst behind her eyes. Her knees weakened, and she would have fallen. But he grabbed her by the hair, throwing her onto the chair. He tied her to it.

She fought to remain conscious, knowing it was her only chance. "I have done nothing to you. Please let me go."

"You may not have done anything, but your death will bring me great satisfaction."

"Please don't do this. I'm begging you." But anything else she might have said was cut off when he shoved a rag in her mouth. Her heartbeat thundered in her ears. She closed her eyes against the hot tears. *She was going to die.*

A splashing sound caught her attention. He stood a mere ten feet from her, tossing gasoline from a can over the floor and walls, across the old packing crates. "It'll be fast." With those parting words, he struck a match and tossed it into a pool of fuel on the floor. His laugh, high and maniacal, filled the room, competing with the roar of the flames. And then came the sound of the metal door crashing closed behind him.

Chapter Eight

Addie pulled against the rope at her wrists, screaming as it bit into her flesh. None of that mattered. She had to escape. Smoke filled the room. Bright orange flames licked over the wooden crates, dancing ever closer to her. She sucked in a breath, but coughs racked her body. The rope binding her wrists tightened with her frantic struggles.

She sobbed for everything she was about to lose. All the things she had never done. The faces of her family flashed through her mind. She tucked her face as far into her shirt as she could, trying to use it to avoid breathing in the acrid smoke. Seconds became hours as the flames drew nearer. She had read somewhere that smoke inhalation would kill you faster than burning in a fire. She hoped so.

In a last desperate attempt, she threw her weight to one side, tipping the chair over. Pain burst through her head where it connected with the concrete floor. But the chair remained intact.

She had given up hope when she heard something other than the crackle of flames. A man's voice whispered, "I won't let him hurt you." He leaned over her and cut the rope holding her bound to the chair.

"We have to get out of here." Strong arms picked her up, carrying her further from the flames and smoke.

Addie turned her face into the solid muscled wall of his chest, sobbing. She tried to say something but couldn't. Her lungs burned with the effort to take in oxygen. In the next moment, the man threw his shoulder against the metal door, and they were out in the bright sunlight, making it impossible to see his face.

He carried her to a small patch of grass, away from the building, and lowered her to the ground. She rolled on her side, coughing and gasping for air. The last thing she heard was the stranger talking to a 9-1-1 operator, giving them the location.

*****

Something cold and wet swiped across her cheek, dragging her back to consciousness. She raised a hand to swat the thing away and felt fur. A chorus of happy yips sounded. The Girls!! She tried to sit up, only to grab her head when the sudden movement brought blinding pain.

"Don't try to move. Help is on the way." Strong hands lowered her back to the ground.

She opened her eyes to peer into dark ones. "How did you find me?"

"That's a long story. Why don't you tell me what happened first?"

"My head hurts." She rubbed at her temple, her eyes widening when she saw the blood on her hand. "I don't feel so good." Nonetheless, she sat up, groaning as she did. Gracey and Lily crowded into her, whimpering.

"It's okay, girls. Come here." Lily pressed into her side, resting her silky muzzle along Addie's shoulder. She felt the occasional swipe of her tongue against her cheek. Gracey stretched out along her leg on the other side.

She looked around the empty, abandoned lot. They were the only two there. She turned back to him. "Where is he?"

He raised an eyebrow. "Who?" Detective Wolfe pulled a pristine handkerchief from his pocket. "Here," he said, offering it to her. "Head wounds bleed a lot."

"Thank you." She pressed it to her temple, closing her eyes against the wave of pain and dizziness that followed. A siren sounded in the distance.

"Tell me who was here with you."

"I don't know."

"You really did bump your head."

"I didn't bump it. That man slammed his fist into it when I kicked him in the knee. I wish I had kicked him somewhere else."

A low chuckle escaped from him. "I'll bet you do. But I don't understand how you got out here. When I drove into the lot and saw that." He waved a hand at the building, which now burned out of control. "I thought you were in there," he all but whispered in a roughened voice.

"I was. Until he rescued me."

"Who? You were lying here alone when I pulled up." He sat on the ground behind her, pulling her back against him. "EMS will be here soon. Just rest."

She wondered at the emotion in his voice. Then she closed her eyes against the pain in her head. "The man from my dreams," she replied before slumping against him.

*****

"I think she's waking up. Somebody get the doctor."

Addie pressed a hand to her head, willing the marching band inside to stop playing. Who was screaming at her like that, and why? She opened her eyes to a squint to find her Aunt Clementine staring at her. She gave a weak smile as proof of life.

"I told you she was awake. Where's that cute doctor?" Clementine bellowed.

"I'll get him," offered Beatrice. "Happy to spend a few moments with that cutie patootie."

"For the love of all that's holy, please stop yelling." She struggled into a semi-sitting position. "Thirsty," she rasped.

Grey smiled from the foot of the bed. "That we can do something about." He walked to the bedside table and poured her a glass of water. He placed a straw in it before handing it to her. "Here you go. Take small sips first. Can't have you getting sick again."

"Should I ask?"

He grinned. "Apparently, you vomited all over the good detective. Would have given anything to see that."

She winced. "I don't remember."

"I'm not surprised. You've been out of it for hours."

She ran an exploratory finger along her temple. "Are those stitches?"

"Yep, but only four. Bastard was apparently wearing a ring when he hit you."

"That explains why it hurt so badly." She took a small sip as directed. When it stayed down, she took another. The cool water felt like nirvana to her parched throat.

"What happened? I only remember bits and pieces."

There was a knock at the door before anyone could answer her. A man in a white coat over navy scrubs entered, Aunt Beatrice on his heels. "You're back with us. That's wonderful. I'm Dr. Barrett.

I admitted you from the emergency department earlier today. It's nice to finally meet you."

She shook the hand he extended. "I'm Adelaide Foster. But you probably already know that."

"She hasn't lost her wit," quipped Grey.

"Good sign," agreed her aunts in unison.

The doctor put her through her paces, shining a light in her eyes, testing reflexes, and asking her a seemingly endless list of questions. When he was finished, she slumped back against the pillows. "So, I'll live?"

"You will indeed. Considering what you've been through, you're very lucky. You do have a concussion, and I understand from your history that it's not your first. So, you know what to do. I'd like to keep you overnight, make sure you're okay. I'll leave you very specific concussion care instructions before you go home. Do you have any questions for me?"

"Are you married, Doctor?"

"Aunt Beatrice!" She felt her cheeks burn and wished the floor would swallow her whole.

He had the grace to laugh. "I'm not. Are you proposing?"

Addie buried her head in her hands. "Do not encourage her. Please."

Grey stood, leaning against the side of her bed. He remained silent yet smirking. He'd been around The Aunties long enough to know when to not get involved.

"Hear that, Addie? He's single."

"Yes, Aunt Beatrice, I heard that." She turned to him. "I'm so sorry. My great aunts think that being single at my age is fatal. Mind you, neither of them ever married."

"I could have, you know," declared Clementine. "But Father didn't approve."

"That's because he ran moonshine. Not at all respectable."

"At least I had a beau."

Dr. Barret held up a hand. "Maybe you didn't hear the part about her head injury. And her need for peace." He stared down the formidable old ladies. "And quiet. Now say goodnight to Ms. Foster. Visiting hours are over."

Grey stepped in, motioning to her aunts. "You heard the good doctor, let's let Addie get some much-needed rest.

"Well, no wonder he's still single," groused Aunt Clementine. She leaned down and kissed Addie's cheek. "Goodnight dear."

Aunt Beatrice bustled over to the bed. She stroked a hand over Addie's hair. "You rest now. And don't worry about the girls. That lovely detective brought them to the house." She winked. "He's single. I asked."

She held in a groan. Eyes drooping, Addie fought sleep long enough to say goodbye. Silence reigned after Grey shuffled them out the door. She fell into a deep sleep.

*****

When she awoke, the room was dark except for a sliver of light coming from a cracked bathroom door. She wasn't sure what had woken her. Possibly her ready to burst bladder. All that IV solution had caught up with her. She debated ringing for a nurse when a sound froze her in place. She wasn't alone in the room. Addie shrank against the pillows. Was her would-be murderer back to finish off the job?

Heart racing, she glanced around the darkened room. Where was he? Had he come alone? Her breath caught in her throat. That's when she noticed a man sleeping in the chair next to her bed. A familiar man. She leaned forward, squinting, to get a better look. And dark brown eyes opened to stare back at her.

"Detective Wolfe?"

The man in question blinked a few times, then rubbed his eyes. "Oh, sorry. I didn't mean to scare you. I, uh, don't usually hang out in hospital rooms of women I barely know."

"All evidence to the contrary."

He ducked his head. "Right. I wanted to make sure you were safe."

"By scaring the life out of me? And isn't that what the guard on the door is for?"

"I needed to know you were safe."

"Oh." Her heart raced at the implications of those seven small words. She cleared her throat. "How is Mike, uh Officer Bradley, by the way? I asked a nurse earlier, but she couldn't tell me anything. Patient privacy and all that."

"He's going to be okay. He was very lucky, considering how badly he screwed up."

"He could have died trying to protect me."

"He should have never left your side."

"He walked fifty feet away to get a soda. I was fine."

"Except you weren't fine, were you? Don't you understand how close you came to dying? Again?" He stood up. Pacing the floor, he was a sight. He'd taken off his jacket at some point in the evening and rolled back his sleeves. His tie was abandoned along the way, and the top two buttons were open. Her mouth dried up, but not out of fear.

"I know exactly how close I came to dying, Detective Wolfe. I was there."

"And I wasn't. I know." He stopped pacing, came closer to her bed, facing her. "I must have missed you by moments." A long breath shuddered out of him. "I pulled into the parking lot to find Mike unconscious on the ground. And your dogs running loose. I didn't know what to think."

"Thank you for saving the girls. I don't know what I would have done if anything had happened to them. How did you know where I was?"

He pulled the chair next to the bed and dropped into it. Leaning his elbows on his knees, his shoulders slumped. "I called in to dispatch to put out an alert on you. And then I heard the call come through for the fire. I had to be sure."

"Where was the man when you got to the warehouse? Didn't you see anything?"

"You asked me that before, right after I found you on the ground. I didn't see anyone there. Then you said the strangest thing. 'The man from my dreams.'"

She bit her bottom lip. Why had she told him that? "Oh. I had just, uh, been slammed in the head."

"You can tell me anything."

And in that moment, she knew she could. There was something in his tone, the softness of his voice. "For the past week or so, maybe a little longer, I've been having dreams. Weird, scary ones. Each one is a little more real, a little more terrifying." She told him about all of them except for the last. And waited for his skepticism. Or worse.

"I can see how they would be scary. But they're kind of vague. What do they have to with the fire and the man that saved you?"

"I didn't tell you about the last one. Last night, I dreamed about the fire, right down to the chair he tied me to." She rubbed at the bandaging covering both wrists. "Before all this started, my dreams were always pleasant, vague, and mostly forgotten before I awoke."

"But these weren't."

She shook her head. "I could taste the acrid smoke on my tongue, feel the heat from the flames." She took a deep breath. "And he was there."

He leaned in closer. "The man who saved you?"

"Yes," she whispered. "Do you think I'm losing my mind?"

One large hand covered hers. She watched as he carefully avoided the IV site. "I don't think that at all. But I am trying to understand."

She exhaled a breath she hadn't realized she was holding. She needed him to believe her. To not think she was crazy. She'd worry about the reason later. "That makes two of us. He appeared in my last two dreams. Always in shadows. Almost like I could sense rather than see him. In the last dream, he said, 'I won't let him hurt you.' He said it to me today. Same voice, same man. I didn't see him. There was too much smoke and then bright sunlight. My head throbbed. He only said those six words to me. The last thing I remember is his calling 9-1-1. I've never heard his voice before."

"They'll have a recording of his voice. That's something." He sat back, staring off into space for a few moments. Looking ponderous.

"What's got your brain in overdrive?"

That got his attention. "You know me so well already?"

She laughed. Her first real one in days. "No. Not at all. But there's a furrow between your eyes. Very serious looking. So, out with it."

Moments ticked by as she waited for him to spill it.

"It keeps coming back to you. International criminals come to middle of Nowhere, North Carolina, to kill *you*. Not one. Not two. But three of them. Two of them are dead. The third one is in the wind. Then mystery man is equally determined to save *you*. You are the common denominator. And yet you still have no idea why?"

She sucked in a breath, staring at him in the dim light. Tears burned her eyes. "After everything I've been through, you still think I'm somehow involved in this." She didn't try to stop the tears from coursing down her face. "Dr. Barret insisted I have peace and quiet, Detective. I don't think he meant that to include you interrogating me. Goodnight." She rolled away from him, pulling the covers up around her neck, and closed her eyes.

He remained in the room for several moments. She could feel his presence behind her. Twice he started to say something. But in the end, he left quietly. When he was gone, she sobbed into her pillow.

Chapter Nine

Addie sat on the stool behind the counter, people watching through her picture window. The summer sun shone high above, drawing people to their little beach town. On a normal day, this was one of her favorite pastimes when traffic in the store slowed. But life had been not been normal in a while. More than a week had passed since that night in the hospital room. She went home the next day with strict instructions from Dr. Barret to rest. And she had.

With her headaches mostly a thing of the past, she returned to work today. And even with Grey hovering like a helicopter mom, it had been the right decision. Never one for idle time, sitting home and being unable to read, watch movies, or surf the 'Net almost drove her mad. Yesterday, she had checked in with a neurologist. With a clean bill of health and orders to ease back into her life, she returned to Smiling Dog Books this morning. Now if only she could have caffeine.

But that was far from her most pressing problem. Her kidnapper remained at large, seemingly vanished. Which explained Officer Burke's presence in her store. The Ocean Grove Police Department, in conjunction with the FBI, had created a task force to find the missing criminal. And they needed her to stay alive long enough to identify him once they caught him.

She had not seen Detective Wolfe again since that night in the hospital. Agents Williams and Fischer questioned her when she had been well enough to do so. They remained in charge of the case, despite the local police department's protest. That was fine with her. Not having to talk to a certain detective again made life easier.

The bell jingled, announcing Grey's return. He had made a coffee run, at least for himself and Officer Burke. Orange juice for the invalid. Yippee!

"I see the stream of nosey town folk has dwindled," he drawled as he handed her a bottle of juice.

"Now, now, Grey. Put away your claws. Those 'folk' buy books. And it's not every day that one of its citizens requires around the clock police babysitting."

"Or ends up the center of international intrigue." He placed some letters next to her on the counter. "Fred says hello. I saw him when I came in. And you're welcome."

She sifted through the mail. "Thank you. I love Fred, but he can be a bit longwinded."

"You're too nice. He's worse than an old woman. And he would have badgered you for details. Not on your first day back. And not when I'm here to stop him." He struck a pose before grabbing books to be shelved.

She stifled a sigh. Grey still had his nose bent out of shape about everything that had gone down. How she had kept him out of it. To. Keep. Him. Safe. Male pride and all that. Nothing she could do about that now. And she would do it again. Her family's safety came first.

She flipped through the few letters, bills, and circulars. Near the bottom, she found a plain white envelope only bearing her printed first name. *Adelaide.* That alone was odd, because no one called her that. She slit it open with shaking hands and found a single piece of plain paper, folded in half. 'You're safe now,' was all it said, printed in black ink.

"Grey!"

He came at a run. "What's wrong?" Officer Burke followed on his heels.

She held it up for them to see.

"What's that supposed to mean?"

"I have no idea."

"Ms. Foster, drop it on the counter, please. No one else touch it."

She dropped it as requested and picked up her phone. By now, Agent Williams was programmed into it. She gave him a brief rundown and hung up. "He just left the police department. He'll be right over."

"Any chance that yummy detective is coming with him?" Grey waggled his brows.

"Funny. Detective Wolfe wants nothing to do with this or with me. He made that clear." The officer put on gloves before sliding the letter and envelope into an evidence bag and

sealing it.

They all stood around the desk, staring at it. Addie wondered what it meant. And who

sent it. She had a guardian angel of sorts. But not knowing who that might be sent a shiver down her spine.

A few minutes later, the agent came through the door. "Let me see it."

The officer's radio sprang to life, and she walked away to answer it.

"I'm sorry about touching it first. I wasn't thinking."

"That's okay." He picked it up off the counter, turning it to read the note. "Safe? Hmmm."

"That's what I thought. I haven't felt safe since this whole thing started."

"There are two ways to look at this. Either it's from the man who rescued you from the fire and he's somehow taken care of the threat, or this is from our missing arms dealer, and he's trying to smoke you out."

"Uh, sir. I may be able to help you with that." Officer Burke approached the counter. "I just received a radio call. They found a dead body in an abandoned car."

"Where?"

"Uh, 210 Dundee Street. That's only ten minutes from here."

He tapped it into his phone. "I've got it. If you could stay here with Ms. Foster, please." He left without another word.

The three stood, looking at each other. Addie barked out a laugh. "Well, that was strange."

"No kidding," Grey added. "I guess I'll go back to tidying up."

The officer nodded. "I'll be over in the comfy corner, enjoying my latte."

Addie felt safer knowing Natalie was here with them. The 'comfy corner', as she called it, was a grouping of armchairs and a low couch that gave customers a place to sit and read. It also afforded a view of the door and entire shop. She might be sipping latte, but Officer Burke had her eye on everything.

The morning passed, with customers coming and going. Her regular group of moms and toddlers came for story hour right after lunch. She loved reading to this age group. They clapped and squealed throughout the story and made an enthusiastic audience. She was finishing up a story of woodland creatures learning to live in harmony, complete with character voices, when the skin on the back of her neck warmed. She continued reading and received a standing ovation from her young fans when she finished.

"You're good with them."

She didn't have to turn to know that he was standing there. "Afternoon, Detective. Is there something you need?" Coward that she was, she kept her back to him.

"Hey, Addie, do you need anything?"

She smiled at Grey. "No, I'm fine, thanks. You remember Detective Wolfe."

His eyes slid up and down the other man, probably to make him uncomfortable. "Hard to forget." He squeezed her hand before walking away.

She took a breath and turned to face him. Damn, still smoking hot in his Heathcliff manner. All dark and brooding. "Here to accuse me of something?"

His face flushed. "Uh, no. But I do need to speak with you." He glanced at the moms, none of whom even tried to hide their curiosity. Or their approval. "May we use your office?"

"Of course." She led the way to the back, head held high, spine straight. He brought out the worst in her. But she would rise above.

She unlocked her office, flipping on a light. Then moved a pile of books from her one visitor chair. "It's a bit tight in here."

He followed her in, shrinking the tiny space further, and took a seat. She did the same, happy to keep the desk in-between them.

"I heard about the note. It makes what I have to tell you even more interesting."

"Does this have to do with the body found this morning?"

"Yes, it does."

"Ah. Agent Williams said he'd let me know."

His mouth tightened the tiniest bit. "Well, I believe the FBI is on their way out of town. They got what they came for." He leaned on her desk. "Ms. Foster, I really am sorry."

"For what?" She knew she was acting like a child, but she wasn't ready to let him off the hook.

He sighed. "I'm very focused on my job. Sometimes to the point of not thinking about how my actions, or words, may affect others. So, I'm sorry if I hurt your feelings."

"If?"

The smallest smile appeared on his face. "You're not going to make this easy for me, are you?"

She bit back a smile. He was so cute when he smiled. Although she found the dark, brooding look appealing also. Probably too much so. "You had a job to do. I get it. So, you found the third guy?" She rubbed at her arms, suddenly chilly in the stuffy office. "The one who kidnapped me?"

"Yes. Kazimir Maric. Single bullet wound through the heart."

"The note I got. It's from whoever saved me from the fire, isn't it?"

"Yes. The 'man from your dreams'."

"Funny. I haven't had anymore."

"That's good, right? It's over now."

"Yes, of course."

"You don't sound so sure."

"It's not that. Three men are dead. Mind you, not nice people. But I still don't know what any of this had to do with me. Why was I almost killed? Twice. Why did a stranger feel obligated to protect me from them?"

"We may never know."

"Great." She stood, walking to the door. "If that's all, I have a store to run. And a life to get back to. Thank you for stopping by to tell me."

He stood, almost on top of her in the small space. A look of longing flashed across his face so fast, she almost missed it. Almost. It made him more human. Almost approachable. Then it was gone. "I'm going to leave Officer Burke here for the rest of the day. Just in case."

"In case of what?"

"I don't know. To make you feel better. Safer."

"Or maybe to make you feel better?" she asked, just to poke the bear.

"Maybe." He held her gaze for another moment, looking as though he wanted to say something else. But he didn't. Just nodded and left.

She stood there long after he left, wondering about him. Trying to figure him out. Trying to figure out why he attracted her so strongly. It had to be the zings.

A hand waved in front of her face. "Earth to Addie."

She had no idea how long Grey had stood in her office. She blinked. "Funny."

"That man has feelings for you. You'd have to be blind to not see that. Not just clueless. Why aren't you doing anything about that?"

"What would you have me do? Ask him out to dinner? Jump him?"

"Yes and yes. Do something, Addie. Otherwise, it's you, me, and a turkey baster."

She burst out laughing, remembering their pact from a drunken night years ago. "But think of the pretty babies we'd have."

"Funny. I still think you and Detective Hottie would have prettier babies. All that dark hair and angst."

"He just figured out I'm not a murderer. Of course, there's still the question of how I am involved in this mess. It may be over, in that the bad guys are all dead, but it won't really be over until I figure that out."

Grey sighed in his usual manner; completely over the top. "You've got that look again."

She patted his shoulder. "Sorry, not sorry. I can't put this behind me until I understand. Grey, three men are dead because of me. I have to know why."

"Three man are dead because of the choices they made, not because of you. Tell me you know that."

"Yes, of course. I didn't personally cause their deaths. But they all died here in Ocean Grove. They all died here because they were after me. Why?"

His smile drooped. "You have a point. So, what are you going to do about it?"

"I have no idea."

The End

Acknowledgments

One day, last April, the amazing Adrienne Dunning ever so casually mentioned to me that she would like to write a cozy mystery. And a lightbulb went off in my head. Followed quickly by the ever-shrinking rational part of my brain shouting, 'You don't have time for that.' And that was that. Until two weeks later. Sitting at a red light. The name Addie Foster popped into my brain. And then all the details poured forth. I literally pulled over and wrote a bunch of details in the notes section of my phone. So, thank you, Adrienne, for that.

Adrienne, Carrie D. Humphrey, and I formed our own mutual support group. I don't know what I'd do without these women!! Whether in person or online or via text, we have each other's backs. And that's a lot in today's crazy world.

To the most patient PA in the world, Margie Greenhow. Where would I be without you??? 'I'm going to try something completely different,' I told her. And she didn't even blink an eye!

For every cover, I have turned to the magic of Rebecca Pau of The Final Wrap. She is so very talented and even more understanding. We've done five Contemporary Romance covers together, so this leap into Cozies was huge. Not that I was worried. She nailed it once again.

My husband, Mark, and my children, Jordan & Lucas mean everything to me. They are my rock. My Mom lost her battle with Alzheimer's, and although it was a long time coming, the loss was more painful than I could have ever imagined. Thank you for your patience as I work my way through my grief.

Last, but not least, thank you to the lovely Lauren Korab for brainstorming titles with me!

How to Help an Indie Author

Reviews, reviews, reviews! Even if you don't fall in love with my books, please take the time to review them on Amazon, Goodreads and/or Book Bub. Reviews are so much more important than you could ever imagine.

Follow me everywhere:

Facebook:

https://www.facebook.com/profile.php?id=100012114317732

Twitter:

https://twitter.com/K_OMalley67

Instagram:

https://www.instagram.com/kimberleyomalley67/

Amazon Author Page:

www.amazon.com/author/kimberleyomalley

Good Reads Profile:

https://www.goodreads.com/author/show/16545063.
Kimberley_O_Malley

Book Bub profile:

https://www.bookbub.com/profile/kimberley-o-malley

Check out my website at www.kimberleyomalley.com

To keep up with me and my books, sign up for my newsletter: http://eepurl.com/dgonEX

Addie Foster Mysteries books 2 and 3 are coming in the next few weeks. Book 2, Dyeing for Change, releases on February 7th. Book 3, Murder by Numbers releases February 28th. Here's a sneak peek of Book 2. Keep in mind, this book is still in the editing process and subject to change.

Excerpt from
Dyeing for Change

Her breath lodged in her throat. She edged through the doorway into a darkened room, not knowing what she'd find there. Everything in her, from her shaky legs to her pounding heartbeat, screamed go back! But she couldn't. Something compelled her to continue. She slid her hand along the wall, searching for a light switch. Finding none, she inched forward on leaden feet. A coppery scent reached her nostrils. Its unpleasant perfume sent icy sweat trickling down her spine. Evil lurked within the darkness. Her foot caught something on the floor. She threw out her arms, wind milling them frantically to keep from falling.

Addie Foster pushed away the memory of last night's dream and played with the straw in her extra Grande, super sweet, over the top iced coffee. She took a sip, cursing her BFF for introducing her to these drinks. They were dangerous to her waistline and her wallet. She fanned herself, thankful for the table's umbrella. The sweltering late summer sun would be brutal otherwise. Yet last night's dream left her chilled.

"Sorry, I'm late," Grey said, joining her at the table. "Some mornings, I just can't pry myself out of that bed."

This was not a good time to bring up the dream. Her first since the men had come to town to kill her in July. She smiled instead. "What you really mean is that Jamie wouldn't let you go." She winked at him. "I can see where the turkey baster may never come into play." She and Greyson Waverly had been friends as long as either could remember. They had a running joke to have a child together if neither married by a certain age.

He took a sip of the drink she'd bought for him. "Can you blame him? I'm fabulous."

She laughed at his outrageous claim. "Yes, you are my friend."

"Jamieson and I are having fun. I wouldn't say he's threatening the turkey baster. At least not this early into it."

She covered his hand with hers, giving it a squeeze. "Well, I like him. And I think you're good together. He puts up with your crap. And besides, I still have several years left of viable eggs."

"Yes, you do. And after that, there's technology."

She pulled a face. "Funny."

"You know I say that with love." He pulled his chair in closer to the table and lowered his voice. "Made any progress?"

"No," she replied in a flat tone. "Six weeks have passed, and I'm no closer to figuring out why those men wanted me dead." She drummed her fingers on the table, her nails making a short tapping sound. Three dangerous criminals from half way across the world had descended upon sleepy, little Ocean Grove, North Carolina, turning her life upside down. They intended to kill her. And almost did. Twice. All three had died, two taken out by a mysterious stranger who had stepped in to save her.

"Not for a lack of trying on your part."

She shook her head, tossing her ebony curls in the process. "I don't know what else to do, Grey. I've looked at it from all angles. It just doesn't make any sense."

"I don't suppose you asked a certain hunky detective for assistance." He wiggled his eyebrows at her.

"Just because you and Jamie are all happy together, doesn't mean the rest of the world has to be."

"I take it that's a no then," he asked, tongue firmly implanted in cheek.

She played with her straw, not sure how to answer. "I haven't seen him since the day the last body was found." Her anonymous benefactor had sent her a note, assuring her she was safe again. "Detective Wolfe wasn't too happy about how things played out."

"He just has his panties in a twist because someone else saved the day. He didn't get to be the hero."

She laughed. "I'm sure that's it." There had been a few odd moments, when he forgot to hide his emotions, that she thought he might be interested. But then the professional façade would drop back into place.

"Just because Detective Hottie hasn't said anything doesn't mean he isn't thinking it. Go for it. What's the worst that could happen?"

She tapped a finger against her chin. "Let's think about that. He could say no. He could laugh at me. He could run screaming from the room."

"Or, he could say yes. Which might be the scariest possibility of all. Then, you'd have to risk your heart."

"You forget that fact that I'm seeing someone. Not sure Noah would appreciate me asking out another man."

"Honey, y'all haven't had sex yet. And you've had five dates, which means you are way past the third date. Besides, Dr. Barrett isn't the guy for you. He's way too nice. And by nice, I mean boring."

"Grey! That's a terrible thing to say. Unlike you, I don't have sex on the first date." She grinned at him. "I'm a lady."

"And I'm easy. Not exactly news. But I noticed you didn't deny the fact that he's boring."

"Noah is not boring. He likes to talk about his work." She slapped a hand over her mouth but couldn't stop the laughter from bubbling out. "Okay, he likes to talk about his work a lot. I can't be the only one not wanting to hear about boil lancing while I'm eating."

"That's just wrong."

"But he's passionate about his work. I admire that." She held up a finger when Grey would have interrupted. "My life has been crazy this summer. I was almost killed. Twice. Some mystery man killed people to protect me. And I have no idea why. So, if Noah is a little less than thrilling, I'm okay with that."

"Adelaide Foster, you better not be crossing your fingers under the table."

She held up both hands, after uncrossing the fingers of one. She really didn't care to lie to her anyone, let alone her BFF. "Noah and I are hanging out, having a little fun. I never said I was going to marry the guy."

"Does he know that? Because I've seen the way he looks at you. You can tell he has images of a white picket fence and 2.5 perfect children running through his head."

"Stop. He and I have been on exactly four official dates, five if you count the time I ran into him in the coffee shop."

"And now for the most important question. Is there a zing? And don't try to tell me you don't know what I'm talking about." He smirked before taking another drink.

She let out a breath, ruffling the curls over her forehead. "There isn't any zing. The last time I felt that was with, well, you know who."

"Detective Hottie, that's who."

"And that should tell you something. First, he thought I murdered someone, then he can't let go of my being at the center of such a mystery. No thanks. There may not be any zings, but Noah is a nice man who cares about me. I owe it to myself to see where this goes. And before you say another word about it, I have to go." She pushed more curls out of her eyes. "This hair isn't going to cut itself."

She gathered her purse, slipping her phone into it. "I have an appointment at Dyeing for Change. And you have to open the store." She stood up and walked around the table. "I'll see you later," she said before kissing his cheek.

"You be careful," he advised.

She pulled a face. "What's the worst that could happen? I've had the same cut for years."

He pursed his lips. "You know better than to put that out into the universe. Especially the way your life is going."

She patted him on the head. "Good thing I'm not superstitious. See you later."

She headed for her appointment. Gwen Tucker, owner of Dyeing for Change, agreed to come in early to cut her hair so that she could get to work. She was great that way, always willing to fit her in when she needed a cut. Addie tended to wait until she was ready to take a pair of scissors to her own hair to make an appointment. She loved her naturally curly hair but freely admitted it had a mind of its own. And right now, she needed Gwen to tame it.

Dyeing to Curl was right in town, only two blocks from the book store, so she decided to walk. One of the many things she loved about Ocean Grove. All the things she needed were right here. Her store, the fabulous coffee place, great little restaurants, and her hair cutter.

Gwen thick New York accent cracked her up. She had shown up in town maybe five years ago, tired of snow and 'months of grey', rented a vacant storefront on Oak Street, and the rest was history. She had mostly an older clientele, the Aunties included. Both Clementine and Beatrice were regular customers, with standing Friday morning appointments for a wash and blow out. Addie knew that her great aunts loved the gossip as much as the personalized treatment they received.

She turned onto Oak Street, smiling at people she passed. Even though it was hot enough to melt, she loved summer. And besides, Gwen always kept it nice and cool in the shop. Reaching the front door of Dyeing for Change, she grabbed the knob to open it. But it was locked. The sign on the door was still turned to closed. Hmmm…

Cupping her hands to see better, Addie peeked inside. She caught a glimpse of Gwen ducking into the back room, so she knocked. And waited. Gwen was known for wearing earbuds and rocking along to eighties hits. She knocked again, harder and longer this time. After a moment, the owner appeared in the door, shaking her head.

"I'm not open yet."

"I know. You were going to cut this messy hair I have before I go to work. Remember?"

Gwen's eyebrows pulled together. "Oh, was that today?" She opened the door, but before Addie could say anything, Gwen pulled her inside. She then poked her head out and looked up and down the street. She relocked the door.

"Are you okay?" The other woman seemed nervous to her. She wondered why but didn't really know her well enough to ask.

"What? I'm fine. Why wouldn't I be? Sorry I forgot. Luckily, I came in early to do inventory." She laughed, but it was high-pitched and sounded forced.

"Ugh. That's the least favorite part of having my own business."

"Agreed. But it has to be done." She jumped when someone slammed a car door out in the street, dropping her keys. "Oh, I'm so clumsy these days." She bent to pick them up. "Why don't you take a seat at one of the sinks. I'll be right there." She scurried into the back room.

Addie watched her go, wondering what was going on with her. Gwen was usually the most laid-back woman she knew. Not today. She shrugged. Gwen would tell her if she wanted. She set her purse on a chair and took the sink next to it. She reclined in it and thought about all she had to do today.

Made in the USA
Columbia, SC
13 January 2019